Andrea Bajani

If You Kept a Record of Sins

TRANSLATED FROM THE ITALIAN BY
Elizabeth Harris

Afterword by Edmund White

archipelago books

Archipelago Books
252 3rd Street #A111,
Brooklyn, NY 11215
www.archipelagobooks.org

Distributed by Penguin Random House
www.penguinrandomhouse.com

Library of Congress Cataloging-In-Publication Data available upon request
Cover photograph © Stephen Gill from *The Pillar*
Book Design: Gopa & Ted2, Inc.

This book was made possible by the New York State Council on the Arts with the
support of Governor Andrew M. Cuomo and the New York State Legislature.

Archipelago Books also gratefully acknowledges the generous support
of the New York City Department of Cultural Affairs, the National Endowment
for the Arts, Lannan Foundation, the Carl Lesnor Family Foundation,
and the Nimick Forbesway Foundation.

PRINTED IN THE UNITED STATES

IF YOU KEPT A RECORD OF SINS

I THINK IT HAPPENED to you, too, the first time you arrived. That a man was there, waiting for you, just past the baggage-claim exit, with your name on a sheet of white paper. And he studied the faces, one by one, trying to guess which face went with his sign. The man waiting for me pressed against the barrier, raising his sign higher than all the others, and those signs waving around made it feel almost like a protest rally. Then we recognized each other; I walked toward him and he folded the sheet of paper over twice and it disappeared into his breast pocket. Your first and last name had been written there, like you were the one who'd arrived and not me who'd come all this way to see you put underground.

W‍E SHOOK HANDS and didn't speak. He'd only told me his name, Christian, and then looked down. The feel of his hand stayed with me, that tough skin, a hand that seemed on loan, it was so disconnected from that gentle, averted face. Welcome to Romania, he said, and picked up my bags. We just stood there a moment, a few meters from the sliding doors, with me hesitating to leave and the doors opening and closing as people walked through. Welcome to Romania, he'd said, while in that Romanian airport, all I saw were Italians rushing by, curt men and women, out of breath, running with their roller bags. The same people I'd flown in with only a few minutes before, the same ones screaming into their phones as soon as the plane came to a halt on the runway, the same ones who kept on screaming inside the shuttle bus, and then disappeared with their carry-ons while I waited for my bag. All these people hurrying, and you were once among them, too.

Christian stood beside me a while, both of us frozen in that transit zone. Then he took the initiative, said, Please follow me, and headed for the exit and slipped through the doors. Seen from behind, wide shoulders swallowing his neck, those hard hands made more sense. I looked up and Christian was gone, had disappeared across the street, and people kept walking by, and the loudspeaker kept announcing Aeroportul Otopeni, then rattling off arrivals and departures in every language on earth. So I walked up to those glass doors, too—the satisfaction of seeing them open just before running into them. And now I was outside, the sun exploded in my face, and this was Romania. I looked for Christian in the midst of all the traffic, but the violent glare on the windshields made it too hard to see to the other side. Then I saw he was next to me, we'd been standing together without realizing it, both of us searching for the other, over there. We started to cross, trying to find gaps in the traffic, weaving through the rows of cars, laying our hands protectively on the hoods. We wandered a bit in the parking lot; Christian didn't remember where he'd put the car. When he saw it, he sped up. The lights flashed with the remote key, and he arranged my bags carefully in the trunk. Next to us was an ancient, beat-up Dacia that looked like it had been there fifty years. The parking lot was filled with these seemingly abandoned cars, like bicycles chained to posts, their owners long dead and people walking past.

He wanted me to sit in the back, said, Please, opening the door. Then for most of the drive he was silent; I stared at his neck, his hairline, I was looking for Romania on him, and for traces of you. Now and then he'd glance at me in the mirror and say, Sorry about your mother. His Italian pronunciation was clear—it was his look while he spoke it that was foreign. His expression was one of mourning, as though with this drive from the airport, your funeral had begun. Christian had been your driver for many years. Every time you landed in Bucharest, he was there at the airport; he waited for you just outside the barrier, and took your bags. Every time, he had you sit in the back; he found something good on the radio for you, and without your saying a word, he took you to your firm. At night he came and picked you up and drove you home. It was the same car as now, your name printed on the side, along with your partner's. You'd sit where I'm sitting now, see what I see now, the city suddenly coming to an end, and us out in the open now, in an unchanging landscape going on for kilometers.

Christian couldn't be over thirty, but he looked much older, gray hair over his ears, small eyes that seemed like candies in paper wrappers, wrinkles radiating from the edges. He drove gripping the wheel, as if he could strong-arm this awful road into submission. He was being deferential—I might be young, but I was still your son. With each pothole, he'd look at me in the rearview and say, Sorry, like it was his fault I had to witness all this disorder. As a result, we went slowly, Christian making small slalom turns, avoiding potholes, and me gripping onto the front seat, laughing, though I couldn't say why. Now and then we passed a horse and cart; Christian would point and raise his eyebrows in a mixture of pride and shame. The countryside was blocked out by a row of sheet-metal warehouses packed together, each with a name at the top like a flag, names that were Italian, French, German, Danish, American. I didn't find yours in that cordon of boxes running on for kilometers, like a wall of cement and tin.

Then I went ahead and leaned back, and Christian turned on the radio, keeping an eye on me in the mirror. I raised the lid on the ashtray, a graveyard of smashed butts inside—your cigarettes—I dropped the lid back down. After a while Christian said, We're almost there. But I didn't know where there was. I'd only gotten a telegram from your partner, from that partner printed next to you on the side of the car. The telegram only included the date of the funeral and a number I'd called about my arrival time at Otopeni Airport. A girl on the other end had told me someone would come pick me up and take me to my Destination. She also said, I'm sorry, Lorenzo, and she said my name like she'd known me a long time.

We left the main road and turned onto a dirt road that cut the countryside in two. Christian turned off the radio. In the distance, a blue building stood in the middle of nowhere, almost like a tin hunting lodge. Two flags hung from the roof above the entryway, the larger, the Italian flag, the smaller one waving beside it, the Juventus banner. Christian looked back at me and said, Here we are, then turned to face forward again. He slowed the car, honked twice, and the gate opened. Here we are, I repeated, and we drove through, the two wings of the gate slowly shutting behind us.

ND SO I finally saw him again, after all these years. While Christian maneuvered around the large SUVs left in the yard, I saw him break away from a small group of workers and come toward us. Christian stopped the car, turned off the engine, and once again he said, Welcome to Romania, with a half-smile, as though Romania wasn't what I'd seen as the airplane descended; it was this cluster of men outside a blue building. Your partner, at a distance, was already holding his hand out and breaking into a wide grin. Welcome to Romania, he said to me as well. Then he introduced himself with his last name, shaking my hand and laying his other on top, for emphasis. Anselmi, he told me, like we'd never met before. We bounced a little, pumping hands, staring each other in the eye like two heads of state who didn't speak the same language. So you're finally seeing the place, he said. Meanwhile, Christian was approaching with my bags. Anselmi pulled his hand free and grabbed Christian's arm to stop him. They spoke briefly, looking at the car, then Christian walked back, opened the trunk, and set the bags inside. We've got a hotel room for you downtown, Anselmi said. He put his arm around my shoulders, in confidence: Sorry about your mother. It was really unexpected.

I know so much about you, he said, voice raised, practically shouting. I have your picture around here somewhere. Then he stretched his arms wide and said, Did you ever imagine it would be so big? I said, Not really, and turned to look at the buildings; at the large vehicles strewn about, windows down; at the loading platforms that were piled high. We're the biggest operation around these parts. Did you land at Otopeni? he asked, looking up at the sky. I nodded. Great—then you saw us. Around here, if you land at the airport, we're the only ones you see. I bet they can even see us from the moon, he said, or from satellites—like the Great Wall of China. They see all this land, and there, smack in the middle, is us. He was shouting, not talking, over the din of pounding metal from the warehouses, the screeches of welding, the workers shouting. As you can see, we're always working, he said, we never stop. Now and then someone came out on a forklift, crossed the yard, and disappeared into the opposite warehouse, then returned more slowly, the forklift loaded with boxes. He kept driving back and forth between these two buildings while your partner told me about all the effort and the glory, and about Romania, this exceptional land, all the desire for redemption, and all the girls here, like you won't find anyplace else on earth. Look, he said, pointing to the forklift driver, before they were hopeless as workers, but just look at them now. These people—we yanked them right out of the Middle Ages.

Then he turned, full of pride, staring after a girl sitting on the steps, That's Monica, he said. Tell me you ever saw a girl like that before. The girl realized we were talking about her, and she smiled and called hello. Look at her over there, Anselmi said, look at that smile. Now watch her come running. And he shouted her name and waved her over. She got to her feet, straightened her skirt, and hurried toward us. If she had a tail, she'd be wagging it, he said, following her with his eyes. When she was beside us, he slipped his arm around her waist. I looked at him, then her. She seemed uncomfortable as she held her hand out to me and said, I'm Monica—we spoke on the phone. She looked tiny next to Anselmi, almost half his size, two twitchy legs poking out from under her skirt, hair pulled up, and eyes so green you barely saw her nose. Anselmi walked off now, saying, She'll take good care of you, and he headed over to the group of workers he'd been with when he first saw us drive in. They'd stood there the whole time, not moving. They'd watched me speaking with Anselmi; it was clear they didn't know who I was, but maybe they saw something of you in my face. I'm sorry, Monica said, her hands fidgeting, and I thanked her. Then I added, Don't worry about it. The two of us were left alone, and not knowing what to say, I stared at the warehouse over her shoulder, while she, embarrassed, looked down at the space between our feet. We stood like that, and the hum of the factory helped this to feel like something other than silence.

CHRISTIAN SAT in the car the whole time, his foot out the open door. Anselmi hadn't said a word to him, and neither had anyone else. Only Monica gave him a vacant hello when she'd walked by, and Christian had looked at her lazily, chin raised. Now and then he took his cellphone from his jacket, opened it mechanically, and stuck it back in his pocket. He was staring past the windshield, like it was the sea out there, and not a metal wall.

Please excuse my Italian, Monica said, watching the forklift driver. She'd spoken so little, I hadn't noticed her Italian. Unfortunately, she said, I never studied—I learned it from him. She said *Him*, meaning Anselmi, assuming a shared familiarity that really only applied to you. What little Italian she did have was from Anselmi, from random words intercepted and then stitched together with other scraps of conversation. Actually, now that she was loosening up some, I realized she also spoke like him, with his same inflections, borrowed terms used from a different stature, her with her twenty-five years carried so lightly, and him with these words spewing violently from his mouth. I could tell that she wanted to break the tension, that she wasn't sure what to say to me, All right, she'd say, and laugh and fidget with her hands, repeating, All right. She asked, Do you like Romania? And I answered that I'd only just arrived. There are ugly things and beautiful things, she continued, like in all countries. Sure, I said. Then she smiled and said, You Italians like Romanian pussy. She said this the same way Anselmi would, his same words, his same inflections. His same solemn tone.

The gate opened and a truck came through. Anselmi directed it toward the back of the yard and looked my way with a proud smile, as if to say, We never stop. The driver stepped down and opened up the back. Two workers climbed on and started handing boxes out to two others, who stacked them on a loading platform. Anselmi stood back, directing this operation at a distance, in case someone was clumsy enough to dirty his dark suit. The unloading complete, he came over and pulled the back door closed, paid the driver, and gave the truck a slap on the way out, like he'd slap a horse on the rump.

Monica left right before Anselmi returned. She said, Excuse me, and ran off, like she'd suddenly remembered something. Come with me, Anselmi said, grabbing hold of my arm, I'll introduce you around—the workers loved her, too. Since I'd arrived, they'd stood together talking quietly. Lula's son, he announced, like I'd popped out of a cake. He's only just arrived from Italy, but he already knows this is the center of the world. He said *This* pointing to the cement we were standing on. As if, again, the center of the world was that warehouse, and not Romania, which only happened to be surrounding it. They all broke out laughing, raucous laughter. You come here, you don't ever leave, Anselmi said. Did you ever ask yourself why your mother didn't come home? Did you ever ask yourself why?

YOU STARTED LEAVING when I was young. The first trip was for pleasure, to go meet some friends who were off trying to strike it rich. You drew the world on a sheet of paper the night before, to show me where you were going. We're here, you said, and tomorrow I'll be right down here, in this spot. You drew a line with a red marker from home to there. It's a bridge, you said, it's like crossing the river to the other side. And under the bridge we colored everything blue; we filled in the water of Europe. Then we taped the picture to the refrigerator, and that's where it stayed for years to come.

At first you weren't gone for very long, a few days, a couple of weeks at most. I waited for you, but I wasn't worried—you don't worry when someone has crossed the river to the other side but then comes back right away. Dad wasn't happy, but he didn't let on: in the morning he took me to school; in the afternoon he came and got me and took me back home and never said a word. When you weren't there, I found a thousand excuses to disappear into the kitchen and get something from the refrigerator. I went just to see that drawing of the world, to run my finger over that red bridge that had sprung up between you and me. Then I'd open the fridge and every time, I thought I'd see you in there, like I'd opened a window. But instead of you, there'd be the usual carton of milk with the cow, the packages of processed cheese, and Dad's cans of beer. Once Dad came into the kitchen while I had my face stuck in the fridge, and he asked me what I was doing; I told him what you always said when you opened the refrigerator. I'm checking to see if we need something from the store.

But then you always came home, and I didn't guard the refrigerator, and Dad regained his voice. The first time you went to Romania, you showed us pictures of your friends. You held out the photos and said, I've never seen people laugh so much. And they certainly were laughing in those photos, but then again, people always laugh in photos. I knew them well, these friends of yours—they used to come over quite a bit with their wives and children. You all would talk into the evening about work, while we sat on the rug in front of the TV, watching and laughing and finally falling asleep on the floor. Then they suddenly stopped coming over, maybe because they'd crossed the river to the other side. I still saw the children at school; your friends' wives would pick them up at the entranceway.

Sometimes after school you took me to the firm because you had work to finish. So I'd wait in your office on the second floor with my school notebooks open and would pass the time going up and down on your swivel chair. Sometimes I'd leave and go out to the mezzanine and lean over the rail. From up there, I'd watch you hurry through the lobby, someone beside you talking, you nodding and at some point, he'd stop. And I liked that to talk with you, people had to walk with you, had to ask to walk along beside you, and then they'd turn and go back the way they came. When it was getting late and I'd finished my homework, I would go out again and sit on the mezzanine, my legs dangling down, and I'd look below, at the florescent lights that kept growing brighter. The few remaining office workers would be wandering around in their shirt sleeves, their ties loosened. Sometimes you'd signal to me, as if to say, Almost done, and I'd answer with a wave of my legs, my hands gripping the rails.

The last to arrive, at night, was your partner. Before that, there was no leaving. When he did arrive, you'd follow him into his office, and you two would shut yourselves in for a while, and I couldn't see or hear you. Sometimes I even fell asleep, my legs through the rails; when I awoke, it felt like I was on a swing. Then you'd find me, after your partner left, and you'd slip my notebooks into my backpack. Call Dad, you'd say, because if I called maybe he wouldn't be angry. So we'd go down the metal stairs and step outside to nightfall, to the empty lot and your car that seemed abandoned, in the middle of nowhere. Want to shift gears? you'd ask in the car. And off we'd go, your foot on the clutch and both my hands on the gearshift. Until we reached home, a bit herky-jerky, the slope to the house the most difficult part. We'd stop in the driveway, and every time you'd say, Be good now, before you turned off the ignition.

THE FIRST TIME I saw where you worked was the day of the press conference. The firm had been open a short while, but first things had to be set up, adjusted, perfected, and then and only then, could you bring in the press and show them how good you were at making people lose weight. You'd phoned journalists to let them know about your machine, they'd been talking about it, and everyone had questions for you. The morning of the press conference you brought me to school, and the entire drive you told me what an important day this was because you were about to reveal something, something you'd never told anyone else. I could tell you wanted to bring me along, but you weren't sure how to handle it with the school. We double-parked and walked up to the gate, you carrying my backpack, me tripping a little over my untied shoe. Then you stopped. You looked at me and said, How 'bout we get out of here? Soon we were back in the car, me laughing, lying flat on the back seat, and you in your sunglasses, saying, Stay down—if anyone sees you, we have to go back.

Your product was an egg as big as a grown man. The top half opened, like a cardboard Easter egg, and then it would close shut, like it had never opened at all. You put fat people in there, so they would sweat, inside and out, once a day. It took three years to get it up and running. At first it was just a design on a big sheet of paper, spread out on the kitchen table. You showed it to us one night after dinner, after going back and forth from the table to the sink, clearing everything away, loading it all into the dishwasher. Then you unrolled the sheet of paper and inside was this egg, like it had just been laid and rolled up in newspaper. Here it is, you said, staring at us, clearly expecting praise. All I asked was, What is it? Dad just nodded, and for a second, you were about to get up and leave. But you really needed our affirmation, and so we spent half the night imagining extremely fat men and women being swallowed up inside the egg and coming out extremely thin. You jotted some numbers down on a notepad beside the drawing, then plugged them into your calculator and told us the result, because losing weight, you said, was a mathematical fact. But this was all at the beginning, the egg was only a drawing spread out on a table in the kitchen, the struggling company focused exclusively on cosmetics, and you and Dad still seemed like a father and a mother.

When you presented the egg to the press that night, three years had gone by. For a time, you even set aside the idea of producing your weight-loss machines. You'd talk on the phone with your partner, late at night, the door to the office half-open and the desk lamp on. I'd roll over in bed to see your shadow flickering in the hall, like you were a flame in the night. But he just couldn't do it, your partner, he couldn't convince you to shelve the egg, and by staying on the phone all night, it's you who won. So when the journalists arrived, it's you who gathered them together and distributed folders and shook everybody's hand. He walked beside you, shook hands with them after you, and looked a bit uncomfortable in this role. I was on your other side, and I didn't know what to do with myself, if I should shake hands, too, or smile, or take off my backpack filled with my schoolbooks and drop it somewhere. In the end I just watched you, followed behind you, went where you went.

When you asked for quiet, everyone turned around. They were on one side, you and your partner on the other, and for a moment, I was there alone, in the middle, still wearing my backpack. You said, Thank you for coming. This feels, for us, like we're about to reveal a secret. Then you waved for everyone to follow. So we left as a group, one after the other walking down the hallways, the employees looking out from their offices and us slipping past like cyclists in a race. After the offices, we walked through the storerooms, after the storerooms, into the courtyard, we were practically running across the courtyard, the last ones not paying attention, bolting to catch up to the group. Are we all here? you asked, standing in front of a white door right off the yard.

Through this door was a lady in a white lab coat, and she greeted everyone with a single wave. You walked over to her, rested your hand on her shoulder, and said, Here it is, pointing to the weight-loss egg the woman stood beside. What you're about to witness is a comparative demonstration. Two models chosen specifically for the occasion, you explained, will undergo two different treatments. The first will utilize a traditional piece of equipment, the second, the weight-loss egg. And two models came in, two fat girls in robes, one sat down on a bench, the other was told to lie down on a cot. The lady doctor wrapped this second fat model in blue elastic bandages and electric wires. Up until yesterday, you told the journalists, this was considered cutting-edge. She pulled a lever and every muscle in the fat model's body trembled in violent, nervous jolts. The model lay there, gripped by convulsions, for ten minutes; you stepped away to take a phone call and the journalists remained seated a short distance from the cot. When the treatment ended, the lady in the lab coat freed the model from the electric wires and measured her belly and thighs, as she'd done prior to pulling the lever. Belly, three centimeters less, thighs, two centimeters, she announced with satisfaction, and the model slipped on her robe and went over to sit on the bench.

But that's nothing, you said, as the other model obediently stepped inside the egg. It's like a second gestation, like entering the world a second time. Then you pushed a button and the top of the egg lowered and slowly swallowed the body, the perplexed smile of the overweight model. You looked at everyone, smiling yourself, and announced a short smoke break, since the machine had to run through its various stages. You opened the door, and everyone left, me at the back, feeling a part of the group now, and you laid your hand on my head and asked, Do you like it? So we all ended up out in the courtyard, nearly everyone lighting their cigarettes before they were actually outside. I stayed on the step, my face pressed to the window to see in. No one else was there, just the egg and the imprisoned model; we'd left her there like she was inside a bread machine. And the girl shut up in the machine didn't realize this, either, that we'd abandoned her to go for a smoke. She was in there smoking on her own, sweating and losing weight and hoping, sooner or later, that she'd once more see the light.

When the egg stopped its spin cycle and you pushed the button to turn it off, the lid rose. And inside was the fat model, shyer than when she'd gone in, with all those faces, the journalists peering down, like she'd just returned from outer space. You gave her a reassuring smile and waved to the others to step away from the egg so she could get out. And out she came, and she put on her slippers and went and lay down on the cot, like a piece of boiled meat that's popped out of the pot and onto the cutting board. The lady in the lab coat measured her belly, thighs, and waist, and said the centimeters lost were considerably more than those of the other model. Incomparable, you said, pressing your fingers down on the model's belly. It's due to the electric ionization of oxygen. Ionized oxygen, you went on, is a highly reactive gas that affects metabolism. It burns fat and helps redistribute it, you said. The redistribution of fat is fundamental to the process of losing weight. With those words, we all turned to the model, to see where it had been redistributed, what had swelled up, her calves, elbows, knuckles, or toes.

YOUR PARTNER OFTEN came for dinner on Tuesday evening. The two of you would go to English class, and when you returned it would be almost ten at night. I waited on the couch in my pajamas, the TV volume down, so I could hear you park. You always arrived in two cars, and you parked them one behind the other in front of the window, and soon I'd hear the key in the lock. After class you spoke English for a while, called each other *Darling*, said *Great* over and over. Your partner greeted me when he came in with *Hi baby*. He hung up his coat in the foyer, got a beer from the fridge, came in, dropped down beside me—I'd bounce and the couch would rock like a swing. Then he'd slap me on the thigh, tell me, *Great*, give me a wink and grab the remote and start surfing channels.

Tuesday evenings Dad was never there; he was traveling for work. We'd eat early, the two of us, then he'd shower, get me into my pajamas, and around nine, he'd leave. Before going, he always set a place for you at the kitchen table, a plate, glass, silverware, and he'd leave a pot with a lid on the stove. When you and your partner arrived, you'd add a plate, a glass, a fork and knife, and you'd pull two packets out of your purse, deli purchases. Then you'd turn on the oven, put it all in, and that empty pot would still be on the stove the following day. When the food was ready, you'd call me; you'd give him a light slap on the shoulder; you'd gather me up in your arms, kiss my hair. Even if I already ate, I had to keep you company; you put out a small plate and a glass, and I watched the two of you saying *Great* over and over. You almost always talked together about work; you were full of smiles, your legs crossed, and him pouring wine in your glass.

The first time I saw you smoke was one of those Tuesday nights. Your partner offered you a cigarette, held out the lighter, and you bowed your head over it, lips pursed. I only saw you smoke on Tuesday nights; other days, you never smoked. One night you two even had me try, watched me cough, him saying, That's how you grow up, *baby*, and you saying, Come on, he's just a little boy. Your partner would look at me and keep laughing, and you'd say, Go watch TV. Then around midnight, the phone always rang, and it was Dad wanting to know how you were. You'd get up from the table, go into your bedroom and shut the door, and come out a little while later. You'd sit next to me on the couch, tell me Dad was at his hotel, give me a kiss and say, That's from him, give me another, and that was yours. Then you'd go back to the table with him, and I'd hear you laughing and talking along with the voices on TV.

Sometimes, you danced after dinner. You both took off your shoes and you swayed back and forth, never leaving the rug. I'd watch you where I lay on the couch, my head nodding from sleep. Show this gentleman how to dance with a lady, you'd say sometimes and pull me off the couch. He'd go flop down in front of the TV and we'd dance a while, me in pajamas and saggy socks and barely coming up to your waist. Follow my steps, you told me, and pressed me into you, my forehead against your stomach, as I looked down, watching to see if my feet were doing their job, or not. Your perfume mixed with cigarettes, alcohol, your partner's aftershave—the smells of Tuesday night. Then I always wound up falling asleep, and when I awoke it was morning, and I was in my bed. You'd be waiting in the kitchen, and out the window, his car would be gone.

Some Tuesday nights he went away early and the two of us stayed up together. Sometimes we went for a drive. We left the house like stowaways, my pajama bottoms showing beneath my windbreaker, slippers on my feet. It's like going back in years, you'd say, when I was really small. It was the last remedy for my insomnia. You'd turn on some music and sing along, and together we'd go up and over the hills, the only car along that stretch of road through the countryside. Sometimes it took very little; other times, we drove for hours. But it always worked, and on the return trip, I never saw home.

WHEN YOU CAME home from your trips, you always brought me souvenirs. You'd enter the house with your partner, drop your bags and shoes just past the doorway, and come find me. Sometimes you were only gone a few days, sometimes weeks. While I plunged face-first into the gift bag, you'd make him an espresso that he tossed back in one gulp, and he'd be out the door again without so much as a goodbye. Then you'd join me on the rug and explain to me where those presents came from and what they were for. You'd pull out the shapka, plop it on your head and start speaking Russian, or some other language I didn't know. We'd stay on that rug for hours, wrestling, me trying to escape on all fours and you pulling me back by the ankles, And where do you think you're going, little man? What I remember about your coming home was the physical contact, a battle ending with both of us sweaty, panting, staring at each other, your eyes amused and mine full of rage. Because it was a game, but it was also my way of telling you that you hadn't been there.

Before you landed for good in Romania, you traveled around the world, introducing your weight-loss egg. You boarded planes, got off planes on the other side of the planet and showed everyone how convenient it was to buy an enormous egg for people to sweat inside. At the airport, a driver would pick you up, open the door for you, take you to your destination. You'd arrive, give a presentation while standing beside the egg, photos, a lunch with reps, then back to the airport. You'd board another plane, leave for another part of the planet, change languages, and talk about ionized oxygen. When you were away a long time, you sent me newspaper clippings, and you were always there, shaking hands with someone, both of you looking into the camera. Other times, you'd stand behind the egg with one of the fat models on-loan, and you'd be smiling together, like a bob-sled team. Dad and I saved all these articles and arranged them in a binder. On the cover I wrote, Mommy? because I didn't know what else to put.

When you came home, you always said, There's so much suffering everywhere I go. But that's exactly why you had to do it, to bring peace of mind to these places, eliminate depression, discomfort, and extra kilos. So you went to Ghana, Lebanon, Bangladesh, Colombia, Peru, China, Zaire, Nicaragua, Romania, Poland, Serbia, other places too. You concentrated on the poorest parts of the world; the people there were full of energy, you said, had a feel for life that was more developed than our own. You said that having devices like yours in places like theirs was almost like bringing them electricity or water or the telephone. In the photos you showed me, there were beauty spas with a lot of people standing outside, watching a few go in. Those are the people, you said, with the money. Not many of them, but they're experienced and want the very best there is. These others, you said, pointing to the crowd outside, are the ones with no money. There's a whole lot of them and they suffer a great deal, poor things. But now they have even more of a reason to get going in life. If they could, you said, they'd all jump inside the egg. Even the thin ones.

So we'd spend our time, when you returned, compiling the catalog of what you'd seen. Sometimes, he'd be in the photos, too, but mostly you'd be alone and smiling, your lip gloss framing your teeth. You made copies for me of some of the better shots, and I used bobby pins to hang them on a fishing net you'd brought back from who knows where. Dad hung the net from my bedroom ceiling, and it draped down to the floor. We also pinned up a photo of the three of us on the balcony staring into the camera, puzzled. Next to my bed was a cardboard cutout of your weight-loss egg that I'd laid claim to. Every time you came back from a trip, after I'd counted my presents, unwrapped them, tried each one out, moved on to the next, I'd gather them all up and carry them to my room, trying not to drop any along the way. Then you'd slip into the shower, saying, You're only home after your first shower. I'd stop just short of the bathroom, one of our little private games. Inside the bathroom, as you undressed, you shot pieces of clothing into the hall, one after the other, like you were firing a laundry cannon.

Then I'd head to my room and drop my plunder on the rug. It grew harder and harder to find any space to put the new souvenirs you'd brought without burying the old. They were from every country, every corner on earth, my room, trip after trip, becoming the world map of your absence.

CHRISTIAN WANTED to bring my bags up to my room. He left them in front of the bed, then went back down. First, though, he showed me the balcony and the facing window, your place, only one floor down from mine. There was a street in between, a few meters of air—it would only take a taut wire and a bit of courage. He asked if I wanted to see you one last time, before they nailed the lid on and lowered you underground. After all this time I couldn't do it, I couldn't say yes. Your face, I'd tried to reconstruct your face ever year on Christmas day, measuring your voice on that single phone call, like a blind man running his hands over someone's features. As the years went by, my image of you wasted away; I'd compare your photo to that voice speaking to me over the phone, and it felt like I'd wound up on a different line. That voice, ever more rasping and heavy—I didn't know what to do with that voice, how to tie it to you. So I stared at your window and sat down on the bed. I just couldn't do it, couldn't go down those stairs, cross the street, see your face and only recognize you as you lay there dead, and never be able to forget you again.

Yet I kept stepping onto the balcony, trying to see you inside your apartment. Behind the slightly parted curtains, there wasn't anyone to see—I was staring at a window, but who knows if they even put you close by. All around was Bucharest, buildings of reinforced concrete crammed together along the boulevard, and a background noise I didn't recognize, as though even the traffic spoke a language other than my own. Some lights were on in your apartment, and I tried to guess which room you used to call from, where you slept. I stared at your place, my elbows on the balcony rail, not wanting to think of it as a furnished mortuary on the seventh floor of an ugly condominium building in downtown Bucharest. I shut the door to the balcony and went and took a long shower, sitting down on the shower floor, legs crossed, drawn up to my chest, forehead against my knees. You've only arrived after your first shower. Afterwards, over there, everything was still the same, the curtains parted, the lights on, and you hidden somewhere, stretched out, eyes to the ceiling.

Then a curtain opened, and I took a step back. It was Christian, who'd seen me out on the balcony but hadn't called over. I watched him walk from room to room like the place was empty, like he'd forgotten something and couldn't remember where. And so I learned where you were, because in front of the last window, he stopped and turned toward me. No signal, barely looking at each other, him in front of you and me in a bathrobe on a balcony. Then he turned his back to me, sat down, and I couldn't see him anymore. Only a thread of smoke slipping through the window, rising toward the eighth floor, unraveling as it went. A nice way to be near you, Christian's method, sitting in a chair, smoking beside you. Over the years you'd taken to smoking with a vengeance, almost out of spite. It began as something on Tuesday evenings, but then it became one of your most steadfast habits. You never went anywhere without three packs in your purse— you found comfort in digging through your purse and discovering them, hiding in there, among your things. And on the phone, the few times we spoke were punctuated by flicks of your lighter and puffs on your cigarette. Then you were coughing and there was nothing more to say.

When I went down, Christian was in the lobby, sitting on a couch waiting for me. He got up to come over, but I signalled he shouldn't. We remained where we were for a moment, not saying anything, not saying that we'd only seen each other a short time before. Then I sat down closer to him than I'd meant to, and we stayed crammed together, on the right side of the couch, neither one of us doing anything to correct that unnatural situation. A waiter came up to us and asked if we wanted something; we didn't order anything. Then

Christian told me, They say the dead go up to heaven, and he glanced at the ceiling, puzzled, not saying anything more, a half-formed thought. He was looking at the ceiling and beyond the ceiling, looking toward your place, as if to say that you'd only managed to die halfway, that while going up, you'd stopped short, on the seventh floor.

CHRISTIAN KEPT GETTING phone calls, trying to arrange the final details for your transport to the cemetery. And judging by his anger, this was no easy task. He'd take the phone from his ear, bend over, hold it to his mouth, and scream. Something I saw your partner do a few hours earlier, barking into the phone, teeth, tongue, palate showing, not wanting any lip. Christian was ranting, slipping in a little Italian, to clarify for the person on the other end. After every call, he looked at me, dejected, and said, Romanians don't know how to work. They got the wrong church, he told me. The one they'd reserved was under construction—having the funeral there was out of the question. Christian looked up at me from the edge of the couch, elbows on his knees, chin in his hands. He looked at me like it was his fault. And what his expression meant was that he was one of them, these Romanians who didn't know how to work. I patted his back, our first physical contact since that handshake in the airport. His back was broad, not what I expected: men are mainly familiar with a woman's back, their father's back.

There was nothing we could do about it, I told him, all we could do was wait and find out when we could have it, this funeral. He looked at me, immersed in a hopelessness all his own, that didn't include me. Then his phone rang again, he stood up to answer, started pacing back and forth across the rugs. I could tell it was your partner by the way Christian looked down, neck planted between his shoulders. He'd try to get a word in, but clearly your partner wasn't letting him, was screaming at him over the phone. Every time Christian walked past the sliding doors, they opened, and for a moment the hotel swelled with noise. Christian would notice and step back, but then he'd forget, walk past them again, the doors would open again, and the lobby swelled with noise. Then I watched him leave, the doors burst open and he was already on the other side, beyond the glass. I watched him walk past me on the sidewalk, so immersed in his phone call, he probably didn't even know he was outside. He might walk a long way, arriving god knows where, like sleepwalkers who suddenly find themselves sitting in the kitchen at four AM. He came back in, a half hour gone by, and said, Funeral, tomorrow. I said, In a different church? No, he answered. Not in a different church. He stubbed his cigarette out in the ashtray, took another from the pack. He turned and looked me in the eye. *Time-out*, he said, making a T with his hands.

Time-out, he repeated, and slid back against the couch. The workers would stop for an hour or so. Enough time to send you to the other world in peace.

THERE'S A TIME in the morning, a single moment when all the city lights go off at once. Like someone getting up in a single room, walking over to a switch, turning it off, then sitting back down. You never know when it's going to happen, you'd tell me. You have to stand by the window and watch—you can't get distracted, can't think—thoughts are like somebody's hands, somebody coming up behind you, hands covering your eyes so you can't see. We did it together one time: I was up early to go to the bathroom, and I found you in the kitchen because you couldn't sleep. You'd watch TV with the volume off, at night. You sat on a stool, staring at the images going by, sometimes falling asleep with your head on your arms, and I'd find you like that in the morning, like you were crying. I came into the kitchen because I saw the light, and you were barefoot, in your bathrobe, laughing. You were so absorbed in your movie, you didn't ask me what I was doing there, in the kitchen, in the middle of the night. Still focused on the television, you gestured to the other stool and I sat down beside you. When the movie was over, you turned to me and said, What're you doing up?

Then you got to your feet, turned off the set, and whispered, Let's go up to the attic, but tomorrow, not a word of this to Dad. We put on our shoes and went up to see the lights go off from the dormer window. We were up there a while, the night before us, sitting under a single blanket on the ledge of the square window. We watched the lights trembling like embers, like a wind shivering over the coals. Then it was finally dawn, and you said, Pay attention, now—don't blink. So I tried to keep my eyes as wide as I could, like when you have to have your picture taken, and you don't want it to come out with your eyes closed. This went on a long time: they couldn't agree when to turn off the lights. I kept my eyes as wide open as I could, using all the muscles of my face and you kept saying, Don't blink, and everything kept staying exactly the same. Then, finally, it happened, and I missed it. You said, So, what'd you think? and I said, I didn't see it. You were quiet a moment, then said, Well, I saw it for you.

Tonight was a night like that, but the eighth floor of the hotel was higher than the old mansard and the window wider. And outside was Bucharest and you were on the other side of the street. I went out on the balcony because I couldn't sleep; I leaned over the parapet wall. There was a light in your window—they must have decided to leave it on, like you do for children afraid of the dark. Christian brought me back to the hotel at midnight; I rang the buzzer, and the doorman took a while to come. Your partner insisted on taking me to dinner, wanted to make up for the problems with the burial. The restaurant was on the terrace of a luxury hotel, in downtown Bucharest, there among the buildings like a gold tooth in the middle of a neglected mouth. When Christian and I arrived, he was already there, sitting at the table with some other people. He got up to greet me, had me sit down beside him. Sorry for what happened, he said, but I've fixed it, same church, tomorrow afternoon. You can fix anything with money, he said, Romanians are crazy for money. All around, on that terrace, small tables identical to our own, everyone Italian, French, German, all of them around tables filled exclusively with entrepreneurs, pioneers, hunters. The only Romanians, those waiting on tables, girls running from table to table, taking orders. Anselmi insisted on speaking Italian to the waitress, I am Italian and I speak Italian. And I know you're only pretending you don't understand me. She answered in English. They think they're so international now, he said after she left. He spoke nonstop, like he had to unspool every word he had in his mouth. I didn't say anything, just looked at Christian the entire meal, begging him with my eyes to get us the hell out of there.

Back in the car, it was almost midnight, him in front again, me behind. The only thing I'd said was I'm going to bed, and Christian stood, too, no explanation needed. Your partner didn't try to keep us, maybe didn't even notice we were leaving. I waved to everyone, though I'd spoken to no one. Near the car, on the sidewalk, was an old man, a scale at his feet and a bowl beside it, a few coins inside. He was standing there, waiting for someone to feel the urge to check his weight. I opened the car door, then closed it, and I turned to the man with his scale. I asked if I could weigh myself, he nodded lazily, and I stepped on. Then I thanked him, dropped a few coins in his bowl, and got in the car.

At my hotel I stayed up, letting the night burn itself out, not sleeping, not doing anything else. Then it was dawn, me on the balcony, your room on the other side of the street, and all around was Bucharest and its embers of light. There's a time in the morning, I thought, when all the lights go off at once, and I stared at your lit window across the way. Slowly, the sky grew brighter, and I kept my eyes wide open so I wouldn't miss it this time. No need to blink. And so I finally saw it. They all went out at once, like someone got up, walked over to a switch, turned it off, then sat back down. Lights off now, the city was reappearing, stepping out from darkness. While in your window, the lamp, no longer needed, stayed on.

CHRISTIAN TOOK ME to see the Ceaușescu Palace. I asked him to think up something to pass the time until that afternoon. I was looking for a bridge between waking up in the hotel and the funeral. Christian was waiting for me in the lobby, sitting as usual on the same couch, as usual on the same end. And he looked like he'd slept in his clothes. Except his jacket, that he must have taken off and set aside. We glanced at each other, not saying anything. I had my roller bag—the truth is, I never unpacked. I'd just pulled out a clean shirt, and stuffed my dirty one inside, squeezing it in, like a crumpled piece of paper to throw away. I wanted to get out of there as soon as possible, deal with your burial, then take the first flight out.

He saw I had my suitcase and gave me a questioning look; I shrugged, hands up, and said, So it goes. Then I sat down on the couch and we drank some espresso, as usual, not talking, sitting right next to each other. He offered me a cigarette, and I smoked along with him, our smoking together, the only place that silent complicity made any sense. Then I said, Christian, and it was the first time I'd said his name. Christian, I said, turning to him, let's go somewhere. He put out his cigarette and nodded. What do you think, I said, what's there to see in Bucharest? He got up, put on his sunglasses, and answered, Nothing. Then corrected himself: Ceaușescu.

So we wound up in front of the People's Palace, after walking the whole length of Bulevardul Unirii, the triumphal main boulevard, with fountains, pools, flowerbeds everywhere. The Ceaușescu Palace in the background, immense, as if right here, the world came to a halt. Christian kept saying, See?, like I could look anyplace else. A boy approached gripping a bunch of shower handsets, started walking beside me, trying to sell me one. He waved them around like snakes, a tangle of hoses cascading to the ground. Every time the boy got close to Christian, he'd angrily chase him away. Sorry, Christian said, when the boy finally walked off with his sheaf of snakes. He apologized a lot, the sort of apology you really can't respond to, not with a Don't worry about it or You should see where I live. The more he apologized, the more I stared straight ahead, at the Ceaușescu Palace. In the end, I did wind up buying one of those shower sets, though. And of course, I told myself, there'll come a day when water starts leaking out the hose. I laid a bill in the boy's hand, and he turned and set his sights on a couple across the street.

A huge crowd of tourists swarmed in front of the People's Palace, gathered in semicircles, all focused on a man or woman holding a sign. The guides mentioned Ceaușescu every few seconds, and every time his name came up, they pointed to the magnificent palace. Christian said, See?, waving toward the clumps of tourists, almost all of them in sunglasses and hats. Ceaușescu, he said, meaning, They're all here for him. The guides spoke, and the tourists listened with growing understanding, expressions indignant, grieving. The guides said Dictator, bloodthirsty, megalomaniac; they said Fear, said Communism, said Thousands dead, said Terror, and the more the atrocities rose, the more the tourists raised their cameras, pointed, and snapped their photos. Christian took off his jacket, draped it over his arm, and now stood in his white, rumpled shirt. He was staring at the Ceaușescu Palace, but his thoughts were someplace else; he was seeing what he was immersed in, not what was there in front of him.

We sat down on the curb, our pants hiked up a bit, our socks showing. Every so often, a stray dog wandered past, then went to lie down in a patch of shade. One came close, looked at us, expressionless, then stretched its muzzle toward Christian, who drove the animal off with his foot, almost kicking it in the snout. He yelled, Disgusting, then said, They're everywhere. Before, it was all little houses around here, he said, houses with little yards. Then Ceaușescu tore it all down to build his concrete monsters and the dogs were left homeless. I don't know if this is actually what happened, he added, but it's what I think happened, anyway. The dog Christian had kicked moved a few meters away and stood watching us, its eyes blank, then came closer. Like Devil dogs, Christian said, kicking at it again until it retreated. His shoes were large, shapeless. I looked away—there's something too intimate about them, about worn-out shoes. We smoked a while, in among the guides saying Criminal, saying Tragedy, saying Violence, and all the others taking their pictures. Aren't you going to take a picture? he asked, disappointed. So I pulled my camera out of my pocket, got up, and pointed it at the building. The Palace was so large it didn't fit inside the frame—god knows what the others were taking pictures of. Christian stood up and said, No, and then, Go over there. He took my camera and pointed to a spot. Then he stepped back, to get the whole building.

And that's the first photo of my trip to you. There's the Ceauşescu Palace, the whole thing, and also, above the building, a piece of sky. Smaller, in the corner, there's me. The only way to tell it's me is because I know it's me. What you see is someone in sunglasses, a showerhead dangling from his hands.

THE FIRST TIME you went to Romania, you came back and said, Poor things, they're in such terrible shape. The truth is, you had been there once before. But you'd flown in and stayed two days, and the fat Romanians seemed like any other fat people in the world. You said it was a form of democracy, your weight-loss machine, that in their underwear, fat people were all alike, Romanians, Bulgarians, Russians, Azerbaijanis, Lebanese, Congolese, Sudanese, Chinese, Poles, Mongolians, Indians, Chileans, Colombians. And it's true: in the photos you showed me, there weren't any real differences. Standing in front of that weight-loss egg, they were all equal. Only the Chinese in the photos were different. Behind the fat Chinese models, there was always a thin Chinese man holding up a sign. It was clear you'd tried to keep him out, but he returned every time, and stepped forward. In one photo, they were actually carrying him away, him and his protest sign. On the sign, in red marker: WHEN FAT PEOPLE LOSE WEIGHT,

THIN PEOPLE DIE. An ancient Chinese proverb. I asked you who he was, that skinny guy with the sign. You said, Nobody.

So except for a few overweight people, you didn't see anything in Romania, the first time. You landed in Bucharest, were shut up for two days inside a Romanian spa, and you flew away again, headed off for demos in other parts of the world. When you returned to Romania, some years later, you went with your partner and an old friend who was moving everything there; the three of you drove. You left early one morning, with two full trucks. Your friends were going to Romania to build living-room suites. They'd built the furniture here, carefully, in a large warehouse just past the train station. Then one morning they got up very early, loaded everything on their trucks, and left for Romania. Your friends' warehouse was where it had always been, past the train station, and every morning I saw it on the way to school. The only difference: the sign on it—FOR RENT—with a contact number.

When you came home from that trip you said, They're more than fifty years behind—they're stuck in the past. The trip, you'd say, was endless, Romania wasn't as close as it seemed by plane. At the border they made you wait a long time. A column of trucks, kilometers long. Italians, Germans, the French, everyone with the same idea at the same moment. In the opposite direction, on the border, you saw a column just as long as yours, Romanians leaving Romania, like missiles launched from the other side of the world. And so you faced each other at the border, two long lines, convoys seeking their fortune, you with your trucks stuffed full of equipment, them with their suitcases tied to the top of their cars and vans. They're coming here, you'd say, in search of the west, because under Ceaușescu, they were locked in a cage.

When you spoke of Romania, you sounded both frightened and amazed. Remember the Wild West? you'd say, well, I saw it, that line of trucks stopped at the border. And I saw you, in that car standing out among the others on the road. And then I saw the vehicles moving, one after the other, slowly, never stopping, going on for hundreds and hundreds of kilometers, raising clouds of dust, the sun on the windshields, windows glazed with dirt. I could see them clearly, the imposing grandeur of those trucks crossing the landscape, riding triumphantly into the sunset, the field hands straightening up, waving their hats as the caravan passed. And I saw them at night, headlights boring holes in the absolute darkness of the countryside, slicing the night in two. And then I saw them, the Romanians, and for me they were like Indians, feathers on their heads, faces impassive, language incomprehensible. I could see them in my mind's eye, these Indians from Romania, one eyebrow raised in suspicion, the other relaxed, everyone on horseback, hatchet in hand, faces covered in warpaint. And I imagined someone even more menacing who turned his horse, a small band of diehard believers behind him, and cupped his hands to his mouth, screaming vengeance, then disappeared on the horizon. They'd sell everything, you said about these strange Indians from Romania. And then I saw them, sliding down from their horses, trying to sell the pendants they wore, their clothes, their own horses, offering up their woman in exchange for a little leniency, a bit of protection. And finally, I saw fires at night, campfires in the fields, meals, music, dancing, and the Romanian Indians spying from the bushes.

That's what it seemed like, that land you described the first time you came home. And your eyes shone, and for a moment I was afraid you wanted to leave, too, like all the others, that you wanted to set off for the Wild West. Then I didn't see any more Indians or campfires or clouds of dust on the road: I only saw you. And I asked if you'd be going away forever. And not even hesitating, you said, No. Then added, At least for now. But that was just a little dig.

BEFORE, YOU HAD a different life, a life in a rich, prestigious family. We'd talk and once in a while, you'd drop snippets in among your other words, like someone else had said them. I'd watch you, ears perked, but then you just kept going like always. So I'd forget, too, until they popped up again in our talks. In that earlier life, you lived in an austere building in the historical center. Hundreds of square meters for the family of a respected notary. Your last name was by the entryway buzzer, beside an imposing front door. Every time we went by, we'd come closer, and you'd point it out, like a strange coincidence, your last name by the buzzer. But you didn't say anything, hand up, pointing, and me wanting us to stop every time. You'd let me look for a moment; we'd be standing down there, you, nervously looking all around. And soon you'd tug me away, and I'd pull on your hand, trying to go back.

You were the wild child of a lustrous family; your parents would laugh and tell their friends you came into this world with a manufacturing defect. They'd throw their arms open, eyebrows raised, and say, Sometimes, one in a thousand comes out wrong. In spite of this, they put you on display at their lively gatherings, had you sing a song, recite a poem, play the piano that stood against one wall, your mother turning the sheet music. Your parents' friends would watch you, tenderness and compassion showing on their faces—one time you jumped into a man's arms, and your father said, Please excuse her. You hardly ever spoke unless someone insisted, because that's how your notorious manufacturing defect showed itself. When you weren't performing, you sat on a chair beside your mother; in one photo your feet don't touch the ground, your arms are crossed over your lace top, a blooming cluster of bows perched on your head. The important thing was not saying a word.

Speaking, in moderation, was left to your brothers, two and four years older than you, but at home, treated like twins. Those two pieces turned out nicely, your father would say. They'd walk, one behind the other, a platoon of two soldiers, both in vests, wandering from the bedroom to the kitchen, the kitchen to the living room, the living room to the bathroom, and if one was on the toilet, the other was brushing his teeth. You'd watch them go past in a line, hair parted to the side, expressions based on your father's. Over time they wound up doing what he did, their feet exactly matching his footprints. He started bringing them to the office when they were little, and you could already see they were mass-produced, though still with a slight, childish intemperance. When they came home from the office, they took off their shoes in the entryway and hung up their coats, one large and two much smaller, but otherwise exactly alike, down to the last button on the inside pocket.

You said they were remote-controlled, that even from a distance, your father directed their every move. One night you were watching TV while I did my homework in the kitchen, and I heard you shouting, It's my brothers. At first I didn't pay any attention, but then you said it again and called me in. I ran to you—you'd never brought up your brothers before—I knew nothing about them. You were sitting straight up on the couch. Meet your uncles. On the screen, two colored robots were attempting to go down a flight of stairs, down the first step, down the second, then rolling down the third. They tried again, down the first step, down the second, arriving at the third, then rolling down. After trying several times, they managed it, even getting to the fourth step, then rolling down. After a few more falls, they got to the fifth, the sixth, and so on, until they'd reached the very bottom. It was a story about intelligent robots, technologically intemperate at first but capable of learning, until, with proper training, they functioned perfectly. You stared at the TV, laughing hysterically, calling them by name, but I heard anger inside that laughter. You threw a couch pillow at the TV, told me to blow them a raspberry. I didn't have to be told twice, and stuck out my tongue.

YOU WERE ALSO married, in that earlier life, to a guy your parents approved of, just like his parents approved of you and your parents. Your mother and father looked very satisfied as the two of you knelt in church, pledging your eternal fidelity, your remote-controlled brothers sitting in the first row, on your father's right, looking dazed and replete. With that guy slipping a ring on your finger, people from pew to pew were saying your manufacturing defect was barely noticeable. Seen from behind, your train cascading over the kneeler and across the marble floor, you seemed like one of the family—the third robot. And then the ceremony finished, with a deliberate kiss for pictures to set on top of family bureaus. The organ swelled to your stepping onto the church square, and then, as was the custom, everything ended with relatives tossing handfuls of rice while you two clung to each other for protection.

Little remains of that time, though, a couple of photographs tossed into a box, among other debris from the past. In one, your two families posing on three steps in front of the church, the men behind, the women below, arms down, holding purses. Then the two of you, the newlyweds, standing at the bottom, you in your bare feet, shoes in one hand, making a face like you knew you were getting yourself into big trouble. While he's playing the groom, standing ramrod straight beside you. In the second saved photograph, the two fathers are smiling into the camera. More like a business merger than a wedding, a handshake between two CEOs. This is what's left of that union, that piece of your life, piled into a box for years, along with school journals, bunches of letters organized according to recipient, and a few practically brand-new wallets that for some reason had been tossed out.

Then everything collapsed in just a few months, with the man your husband found in your bed one afternoon, and then your father's note on office letterhead, saying that you were a disgrace, that he no longer considered you family. It all happened so quickly: in a matter of days, you were kicked out of two homes, the one you'd established with your husband and the one you were born in, grew up in, with your remote-controlled brothers. And so you wound up parked in a place your father let you have for a few months, just because the others didn't want to see you homeless.

You were also pregnant, by that man your husband found in your bed, who'd then disappeared in a cloud of dust. You called him only to let him know you were pregnant, reassuring him that you didn't expect him to be a father. You didn't tell your parents, just found a way to be out of that place of theirs before they noticed you were showing and had something to say about it. That man wound up at the hospital after everything was over, you lying on your side, the purple infant screaming and grinding his hands and feet against you. He looked at you, embarrassed, not sure what to do, what to say or how to say it. He'd brought you flowers and set them on the nightstand. He turned toward the bed, hands behind his back, too young not to be curious about a newborn but too scared to hold him. After a while he left, and that was the last of him. But before going, he asked if you wanted his last name for your son, and you smiled and said, Whatever you think, wanting to make him feel better. And so he signed his last name and left it there, like a lizard leaves its tail and scuttles off somewhere to grow it back.

That's how it ended, your life from before, with a crushed tail, a few photos, and a bunch of stuff crammed into boxes and tucked away. What remained was your last name on a buzzer for us to see as we walked by. And then there was me, entering after everything had already happened. Looking around, grabbing hold of the last name I'd found.

DAD ARRIVED when I was three. You were sitting on one side of me, him on the other, and I didn't know where to look. He laid a hand on my head, told me, Hi, Lorenzo, and I turned to you. You smiled and said, This is your dad, to encourage me. I looked at him, then back at you, and keeping my eyes on you, I slowly said, Hi, Dad. Then you said, Good boy, and you both started to laugh, and I laughed, too. So Dad was suddenly my dad, though I hadn't asked for this and you hadn't mentioned or promised his arrival. Up to then, no one had asked about my dad, and I never brought it up with you. And that last name I bore was something of no real importance, like the color of my hair, the shape of my eyes and hands.

Dad came into our home slowly, first just once in a while, then bit by bit, he stayed more often, until he finally hung up his clothes in your bedroom. In the summer, we'd wait for him outside by the front gate, two bags on the ground and me sitting on the sidewalk. He'd pull up, get out of the car, load the bags, and we'd head to the beach. Every time I saw him getting out of that tiny car, I'd wonder how he fit, with him so big. He'd step out like he was unfolding, then inflating. Dad had white hair from the first day I saw him, and a long, soft beard. His image blended fathers with grandfathers—I'd never had either and now found both in our home. He didn't talk much; he listened to you quite a bit while he sat on the couch, never shifting, and you getting up constantly and pacing around the room. His calm furnished our entire home; when he was around, our movements were slower, like astronauts on the moon. He'd sometimes lay his hand on your head, like he'd done with me that first day. I never understood this, but it felt good, that big hand I fit inside completely. You two would also fight, and when you did, you'd scream in his face, and he'd stare at you, silent, not moving, while you pounded his chest with your fists.

At night the three of us watched TV together, you and me on the couch, Dad in the easy chair. Sometimes you'd look over, to check that he was still there, his stillness. And you never managed to follow what was on, you were always distracted by everything around you. Especially me. You'd bring your face close to mine and slowly whisper in my ear, and it tickled so I couldn't listen. I'd crack up and hide behind my hands. You'd comment on everything happening on the screen, until neither one of us was watching anymore. Sometimes we fell asleep together, me curled on top of you. Dad would wait for the movie to end, then put us both to bed and everything back in its place, what you and I had thrown around; then he'd join you in your bed. Other times we'd stay up playing until late, Dad going to bed earlier, leaving us there with a kiss on the forehead. And even after he left, something of his calm would remain in the room a while, like heat left on a chair, when the only vestige of the body is a rumpled cushion.

It was only at night that I heard him. I'd fall asleep and wake to his snoring on the other side of the wall. He'd snore and it didn't even seem like him—that noise he made had nothing to do with his face. Hearing him snore, I was convinced someone else was sleeping in there, who left again the next morning. I once even forced myself to go check; I slipped inside your room. And there he was, in bed, and there beside him, you were lying with your eyes open, watching me come in, and you put your finger to your lips. I walked around the bed and right up to Dad, stood on tiptoe, looking at him, up close. That noise he made was different from his voice and even standing right in front of him, I couldn't believe that was actually him, that sound coming out. Then I went over to your side; you gestured, with your eyes too, that I should keep my voice down. Dad rolled over, and I instinctively ducked so he wouldn't see me. But he didn't wake up, just started snoring again, up at the ceiling, instead of to the side.

Amazed, I looked at you, and you gazed upward, to the heavens. Then we started laughing, softly, and the more I laughed the more you laughed and waved for me to be quiet.

YOU ONCE TOLD me, You know what, I'm going to take you to meet your grandparents. They'd learned of my birth from someone who saw you pushing my stroller. I was a few months old; your mother sent you a telegram saying she knew, congratulations, stop, and she'd signed it with her first name. For many years that telegram was folded up in the side pocket of the stroller, and we'd go out, you pushing me all over the place, like a vacuum cleaner. I pulled that letter out years later, the stroller put to rest in the garage, and me in there looking for something else entirely. At that point, the telegram wasn't legible, just a piece left of the congratulations and that final stop with her first name. When you decided we'd go see my grandparents, we were dressed to the hilt. You made me take a bath, ironed my shirt, and rubbed some sticky stuff through my hair to make it stand up in spikes. In front of the mirror, you broke out laughing, seeing me with my hair at attention, and I felt bad and mussed it up, to show you I was annoyed.

You were sure that they'd welcome you back, if only for an hour, if you arrived hand in hand with a child, that rancor fades with time. They'd never looked me in the eye; the only thing they knew about me, heard indirectly, was that I'd come into the world. All I knew was that your parents had stopped talking to you, that my grandmother wrote a letter when I was born, so you said, and that I had two remote-controlled uncles who tried to go down the stairs but after a few steps started rolling down like sacks of potatoes. I knew nothing about my grandfather—actually, I thought he was dead. But you told me, Come on—let's surprise them. Just wait—they'll be so happy to see how much you've grown.

But they weren't particularly happy. We arrived at the front door to their building just before lunchtime. We stepped back a few meters from the balcony, looked up, and you said, They're home. The windows were open, and we could hear music. You said, The top floor, and I tilted my head back so far I felt dizzy, both of us looking up like it was the first time we'd seen the sky. Your grandfather, you said, is always listening to music. He's a bit hard of hearing—he plays his music so loud, it carries all the way across the city. So my grandfather was up there, too, and music spilling from his windows, carrying all the way across the city. When we go up, you said, Tell them hello the way I taught you. You have to say: Hello, Grandpa, hello, Grandma, how are you? Your voice was trembling as you spoke—between the two of us, you were the more nervous—you were wringing your hands. Say it, you insisted, and I said, Hello, Grandpa, hello, Grandma, how are you.

I was ready; we rang the buzzer. They answered after a short while, a scratchy, intercom voice, my grandfather's music from the windows, suddenly softer. You gave your first and last name, explained you were the owners' daughter, that you were downstairs with your son who wanted to say hello to his grandparents. The voice asked you to wait a moment. Nervous, you told me, It's the maid, the same one they had when I lived here. Then you looked at me and said, softly, Be good, now, and I said, softly, Hello, Grandpa, hello, Grandma, how are you? There was another voice on the intercom, different from the last, saying, Hello, Lula, how are you?, as the music returned at the window. You bent down over me, then said, Fine, fine, we were just passing by. My grandmother was silent, the music briefly went down, then was blaring all the way across the city. Listen, Lula, she said, we're so sorry, but we're expecting company. Then, after a moment: It's been a pleasure though. You answered, Oh, sure. I just wanted you to meet my son—he wanted to say hello. Then you told me, Say hello to your grandma, and I said, Hello, Grandma, how are you?, staring up at the tiny holes in the intercom, feeling my face grow red. Your mom answered, Hello, child, even sounding a little affectionate. What's your name?, and I said, Lorenzo, and she said, What a

73

handsome name. You must be a handsome boy. You said, Of course he's a handsome boy, if you let us come up, I'll introduce him to you, just a minute, and then we'll head out—we're in a hurry ourselves.

But she didn't let us come up; people were starting to arrive. Perhaps another time, perhaps try phoning first. She also said, You haven't changed. Then she said your father would have loved to come talk to you over the intercom, but he simply couldn't—he was too busy getting ready. You said, That's all right—perhaps another time. You whispered to me, Say goodbye to your grandmother, and I said, Goodbye, face tilted toward the tiny holes in the intercom. She answered, Goodbye, Lorenzo, we'll see each other soon. Now make sure to look after your mom. Then she said goodbye to you, too, a hurried goodbye, to cut off the conversation, as though you'd seen each other only recently.

That was your grandmother, you said, grabbing my hand to leave. I asked, What's she like? You said, I don't know. Then we walked off, and we didn't look up at those windows again.

WHAT AN UGLY end they arranged for you, in that church with its scaffolding, the sour smell of paint and broken plaster. Of the few people who'd come, some were standing, some sitting in the four pews they'd left us. The bricklayers were at the back of the nave, leaning against the joists, hats in hand, eyes averted, the gestures of people who didn't want to be there but were forced to, by contract.

They delivered you in a van, after they'd nailed you into your coffin inside your apartment and handed you over to the funeral home and its bustling, bloated bureaucracy. The bodies of the dead are airtight because tailors devote themselves to plugging all the holes. This is where you truly die, when the body no longer has its openings. You're plugged up so you won't fester, so the body won't release its own fluids. They even take away your odors, your smoke signals, and they soundproof you with a generous, posthumous stench. They shut you in a box before you're done inside, when the last orifice is finally stuffed with god knows what sort of condiment. In a little while you'll be a coffin with another coffin inside, a nice Matryoshka doll all set for the hereafter. But now that you're wrapped in cellophane, you're no longer a human being. Thank god there's someone who takes the trouble to work on you when you're dead, to turn you into a baby-doll who doesn't sweat, doesn't bleed, and has the good manners not to let any crap seep out her rear. Now that you've become a doll, they can dress you as they please. They slip your arms through sleeves and cut your toenails before binding your feet in stockings more appropriate to the occasion of being deceased. Someone lifts your head and brushes back your hair, like a child and her Barbie. At last you're cut off from the outside world and ready to hop onto the van and go and be prayed to in church, and then burn for all of eternity. You're ready now, and shut up in that coffin, you've become the black box of yourself.

And pulling you out was handled badly, too, pulling that coffin from the van. They whipped the van around on the square, backed up, deep into the mouth of the church. Then they leapt down and unloaded you with gusto, like a new cupboard. They even asked for a couple of signatures, like any good deliveryman. Never mind saying please and thank you, though, with all the dents in the merchandise. When they spat you out of the van, I was there to see you come out in that new crate where you'd been packed away. The others stood further back: your partner, Monica, and some other people I'd never seen before standing on one side, and Christian on the other. They let me walk forward on my own. I came to meet you, when for years all I'd done was wait for you to return. They stood there, your partner, mourning in a pair of sunglasses, and the others, not knowing what to do with their hands, what their expressions should hold when faced with mine. The church square was white in the sun, not the slightest breeze, only the crackling of gravel underfoot as those carrying you rushed forward. Everyone watching like you were somebody else's concern, like I was the only rightful recipient of that wooden box, and they were there waiting on other deliveries, other business to attend to. Then they loaded you onto a metal gurney, to wheel you into church, dead, like a sick person is wheeled into a hospital. They pushed you, and I came after, and soon I heard the others as well.

They left you in the middle of the church for a while, the workers hammering at the walls a few last times, the priest arranging his vestments, the others taking their seats. I sat down, too, on the nylon drop-cloth laid over the pew to protect it from paint. I sat down by a man I'd never seen before, a man there for you. His sweating, his strong aftershave made him that much more of a stranger. I looked at you, there in the middle of all that turmoil, as if this were a dress rehearsal. Participating in a funeral and not even knowing how the person died, that's not something I'd ever done before, and now it was happening with you. It felt like a burial with a missing body, an empty coffin hauled into church to stand in for the corpse.

They'd found a priest who knew some Italian, to send you to the other world. When he finished straightening up the altar, he signaled he was ready. The workers stopped, and it slowly grew quiet. He couldn't pronounce your name properly, and every time he stumbled over it, he'd pat his hip to get back on track. Then a phone rang, everyone turning to look at the bricklayer who was whispering, hand over his phone, the priest, quiet, until the man ended his call. Then the priest went back to what he was reading, I heard him say, If you kept a record of sins—but he had to stop, was suddenly coughing. If you kept a record of sins, he repeated, turning red, as if that line itself had cut him off. If you kept a record of sins, he said, now growing hoarse, If you kept a record of sins, oh Lord, oh Lord, who could stand? But I couldn't listen, my head soaked in the smell of aftershave and paint, your mispronounced name and those sunglasses, even in church.

After the priest told us to go in peace, they rushed to load you on your gurney, to shove you back in the van and then in the furnace, like you'd wanted. But I didn't follow you down there, I left that to your partner and the others. I shook a few hands, kissed a few cheeks, and walked away. I watched them leaving, one after the other, first the van, then the procession of SUVs. A short while later, Christian pulled up next to me, rolled down his window, not speaking, staring straight ahead. I walked around the car, opened the door, and slipped in beside him.

THE TELEPHONE WOKE me, it was noon, the girl at reception telling me it was your partner. *Mr. Anselmi*, she said, and then his voice was on the phone, mid-phrase, unaware I hadn't been listening. Something you did, too, this jumping in right when someone answered—you'd shoot forward like a dog after a gun fires. I told him I was sleeping and hadn't realized the time—I'd stayed up late watching TV. And the TV was still on; it was hard to see anything with the sun, but there was a thicket of voices blaring at the foot of the bed. Anselmi was driving, god knows where he'd put the phone, with him telling me what he'd done and where he was going. I heard music, him screaming at a distance. Then he paused, said, Hold on—there's someone. I heard the car door open, close; I was alone in the car listening to him making more noise. Then he got back in and said, Me again—just want you to know Monica's picking you up.

When I came down, I saw her on the other side of the street, in Anselmi's enormous SUV. She waved and I crossed over and climbed in. At the funeral, she'd come dressed up like a lady, heels, sunglasses, purse dangling off her arm, and holding onto Anselmi's elbow. Now she was wearing jeans, a T-shirt, sneakers, was back to being twenty-five. She smiled and said, Did you get some sleep? Not much, I said. Then we drove off, at first a bit jerky, with her trying to tame that giant bucking mule of a car and me fastening my seatbelt. She drove looking a little worried, a little proud, afraid to dent it, proud to be in the driver's seat of a car like that. Anselmi had said on the phone, Just watch her, driving my car—she thinks she's a queen. Monica was a nervous driver, it was clear she was checking her every move. But when someone in front of us suddenly slowed down, she got nasty, laid on the horn, and she'd seemed so gentle before. She ranted, screamed, What an esshull, then out the window, Esshull. Lips pressed together, white with rage. But when a song she liked came on the radio, she was suddenly singing in a thin voice, everything forgotten, the car, me beside her, the traffic of downtown Bucharest. Even Anselmi. And her voice turned fluid, her eyes grew wide.

We have to stop at Anselmi's, she said. I want to get you your mom's keys, and it felt strange hearing this in her Italian, violated and soiled by Anselmi's coarseness, this fragment of tenderness: Your mom. And I thanked her, more for this, I think, than for keeping my mother's keys. In downtown Bucharest, impossible to move, a flood of cars at the traffic lights, with us above everyone else, in that enormous vehicle. Your mom, Monica said, she was so alone. I didn't look at her, just changed the station, flipping through them a good while, and I turned up the volume. I knew she wanted to talk, was looking for a way in. Anselmi, she started to say, but I cranked the volume even higher. Monica held up her hands. Okay, I get it, she shouted. We drove past the Ceaușescu Palace, and she said, Have you seen it? You should take a picture. I told her I already had one, a picture, that Christian had already taken one of me and the Palace. Then her phone rang, it was Anselmi, wanting to know if we were already there, if we'd gotten the keys, if I liked his place, what I wanted to do that day. When she hung up, she looked over at me and sighed and rolled her eyes. She said, He can be a pain sometimes. Then she turned up the music, a song she liked. She said, It's Romanian, but famous—you know it? And she started swaying in her seat, bouncing around, beating time on the steering wheel.

We parked the car, right tires up on the sidewalk. We're here, she said. As we approached the front door, Monica looked up, so I would, too. It's on the top floor, she said, you can see the whole city. And I looked up, to the very top. It was so tall, this building, that I had to tilt my head way back to see up there—I felt like I was falling. It seems taller from down here, she said, it's not actually that scary, and she laughed. A dog lay stretched across the entranceway, its fur dirty, in pretty rough shape. Monica poked at the dog with her shoe, and it shifted a little to the side, then went back to sleep. Monica typed in the access code on the intercom, we heard the door unlock, and went in. While we were waiting for the elevator, she gathered the envelopes and fliers from the mailbox. There were two last names on the mailbox; one was Anselmi's. The other, a line drawn through it in marker, was yours.

S o, do you like Bucharest? Monica asked as we stood on the balcony. No, I said, my back to the wall, trying to keep from feeling dizzy. She was looking at me and laughing, You're white as a sheet. She smiled, her back to the railing. People who aren't afraid of heights aren't constantly thinking the railing might collapse. She said, You know the only thing higher than us?—that—and she pointed to the Intercontinental Hotel, like a mountain in the distance. I took a few cautious steps toward the railing. Come on, Monica said, holding out her hand. You think I'm funny? I asked, grabbing onto her hand, and she said, A little. I stopped a meter away—I've always been afraid of getting too close— my legs might just take over and make the leap for me. That square over there, she said, is where the revolution happened; she was pointing to an open space between the buildings. Ceaușescu escaped by helicopter, she said, eyes shining, like Ceaușescu was some kind of superhero. They're gross, she said, pointing to the long parade of barrack-style buildings in view. I wasn't sure if she was expecting me to agree with her or not, as if she'd said this to convince herself that they were truly ugly. Yeah, they're ugly, I said, and this seemed to reassure her.

Elbows on the railing, she said, It's Communism, and this sounded questioning as well. Those blocks weren't there before—he tore everything down, she said, with a slicing motion.

Anselmi's apartment was endless, a bunch of small rooms and a hallway filled with light. In the dining room, a wall entirely of glass, showing only sky. I had to come closer to see the city below. We hadn't even entered the apartment before the phone started ringing—we heard it behind the door, and Monica working the lock. It was Anselmi, wanting to know what I thought of the place, and Monica told him we'd just come in. So after we went out on the balcony, Monica called him back, told him, He likes it a lot, then she asked about the keys because she couldn't find them. When she hung up, she opened a drawer, pulled out a bunch of keys, and handed them over. Your mom's keys, she said. She sat down on the armrest of an easy chair, then threw her arms open, saying, Romanians just don't have apartments like this—you like it? She'd already told Anselmi I did; now she wanted to hear it from me. Sure, I told her, very nice. Thanks, she said, then smiled and dropped into the chair with seeming abandon, like a paratrooper plunging out of a plane. Next to the high window, in a vertical line, were framed photographs, one after the other, almost to the floor. Almost all of them, with you in the picture. I think they were of the factory opening, and you were like I remembered, a touch of lipstick, skirt just below your knees, and that seductive expression, somewhere between amazement and teasing. They were all taken at the factory entrance, flags lowered, land all around and curious onlookers at a distance, someone pointing at you two. Even Christian was there, with a smile I'd never seen on him before. In two photos your partner stood on his own—you weren't there now. They had to be later pictures: Anselmi's face was puffier, his hair thinner. He was shaking hands with someone who looked like an ambassador. Then a little above these was a picture of Monica, dressed up like a lady.

She leapt out of her chair: Fuck—the washer—Anselmi's going to kill me. Sorry, she said, for her panicked reaction. Soon she was rushing by with a basket of laundry, saying, Follow me, and we went out to the balcony. Their clothes were jumbled in the basket, a tangle of shirts, socks, and pants. Monica rushed to hang them to dry, saying, It's really late. Inside the phone kept ringing, and every time, Monica snorted, raced in, returning shortly, and every time, it was Anselmi. Finally she gave me a pleading look, said, Would you mind? So I found myself out on the balcony alone, digging through clothes in a laundry basket, pulling out their T-shirts, their underwear. Using the clothespins in a nylon bag attached to the clothesline, I hung up Anselmi's boxers, Monica's bras, holding them with just the tips of my fingers, and a sense of violated privacy—mine, not theirs. The limp socks, toes bunched, the wrinkled underwear, Anselmi's shirts on the line that still seemed to hold something of his shape, Monica's colored T-shirts, so small, like a little girl's, and then there were her g-strings that had nothing to do with a little girl. I hung their clothes and thought about the photos that no longer included you. And then I saw Monica through the glass door; she was on the phone, hunched over a small table, receiver propped up with her shoulder, a pencil between her teeth, occasionally jotting something down. I slipped my hand in my pocket and found your keys. I'm always surprised how heavy, how bulky keys can be when they're not mine. There was a little tag, and an address: Bulevardul Carol I n. 23. I turned, and Monica was beside me. Thanks, she said about the clothes. Then pointing to the keys in my hand, she asked, You want to go to her apartment? No, I told her, but I did want to get out of there.

YOU OFTEN SPOKE of Viarengo, but when you did I bet you you never thought he'd be the one to handle your burial. You'd say, His whole life he's dealt with the dead, but you'd never think it to look at him. When Monica dropped me off by the road, Viarengo was already on the other side, waiting for me. He held his hand up in greeting, Monica answered with a wave, then raised a cloud of dust as she drove away. We stood like that, Viarengo on one side, me on the other, surrounded by fields and sunshine. The road led here, to us, then led away again, and me and Viarengo standing there, the only ones beyond the light poles to break that flatness. We stood like this a short while, as if waiting for a boat so we could cross. Viarengo smiled at me, one hand in his pocket, the other shading his head. He said, Welcome, then walked out to meet me just as I decided to cross over myself. We shook hands in the middle of the road, then he pulled me into a hug. I let him, a debt of gratitude. While he hugged me, I looked down the road, to make sure no one was coming. He said, You're the first one out here today.

So I finally met Viarengo. We'd seen each other at the funeral, but he kept to himself, only coming closer when you arrived, when they pulled you out of the van. He walked past me, not saying a word, to help the men who were unloading you. One of them, hand slipping, lost his grip, and Viarengo shoved his shoulder in underneath. Then they set you down carefully on the metal gurney, and he caressed the wooden box, unthinking, his hand sliding back and forth for a while. Then he walked off, and I didn't see him again. Now he was standing here in front of me, just the two of us, the burnt fields all around and four buildings behind him. He took my elbow, and we walked along the dirt road white with sun. Viarengo was sunburnt and wore a cock-eyed baseball cap, as though the coffins he made were farm animals, not boxes preparing for darkness, food for worms. He pointed to the outbuildings, the machinery, and the fields: this was his ranch. He held out his arms as if everything around was his, not just those four buildings, the parked trucks, the forklift drivers going in and out of the warehouses, as if everything in view was his, to the very end, to the last fields fading into haze. While we walked, Viarengo would occasionally go say something to one of the workers, would pat him on the neck, then come back to me. They're good guys, he'd say.

You know, it wasn't easy, he told me, and I thought he was talking about you. So I nodded, like it was something said under the circumstances, so my response would be appropriate under the circumstances as well. I had to teach them everything about these, he said, they barely knew what it was—a coffin. When I arrived, Viarengo continued, what a mess. I thought, Man, look what Communism's done to them. The first few months, they just stood around, staring like monkeys in a tree, and me building coffins day and night. Getting three hours of sleep. Then when I had enough coffins, we loaded them up on a truck and drove around selling them, me, a couple of guys, and that truck you see over there. But after a time, Viarengo told me, there were two hundred men lucky enough to have a trade, plus all that land I saw. In the end, they're hard workers. They understand a job takes sweat. In Italy, he said, this sort of thing just wouldn't be possible. There are places where you can make miracles happen, and others where you just pass the time waiting for one to occur. He suddenly stopped. Why do you think your mom came all this way? he asked and looked at me. I said, I don't know.

Take a look and tell me what you think, he said, as he rounded the corner of the last building. There before us was a meadow, and in the grass, a long stretch of coffins, grazing in perfect order. Hundreds of coffins laid in the sun, one after the other, like a battalion of dead soldiers, killed god knows where. They're all of the finest quality, he said. Same goes for the one I built for your mother, he added. Then he sat down in the grass and said, She used to come out here all the time—she liked it here. You know, in the end, they're just boxes like any other boxes, meant for putting things in order, putting things into and taking them out again someplace else. Only inside these, you put the bodies of people no longer able to put things in order themselves. You know what, he said, jumping up, there's something your mother loved to do. He gestured for me to get up as well, and he led me over to the warehouse entrance, where five young guys stood around an empty coffin. Then one of them climbed in and lay down, the others laughing. They do it to check the handles, Viarengo said, though it's not really necessary. They like to, though—they're good kids. Then they put the lid on and lifted the coffin by the handles, with the other guy inside. Your mom liked doing this, too, he said, after the boy had stepped from the coffin. She'd say, Let's see what dying's like, and then she'd start laughing. She'd get inside in her skirt and heels and lipstick, and the boys would raise her up in the air.

I stepped into it like I would a tub. I sat down and lay back. And I felt like laughing too, that after so much time, I was once again playing with you. They lowered the lid, and I closed my eyes, wanting to be alone in the dark. And then I heard nothing at all, not one voice, not one sound. I opened my eyes and it was completely dark like before, just the strong smell of wood, as if they'd shut me up inside a tree. For a time, it was entirely silent—perhaps they'd forgotten about me. I didn't want to move—there's no moving when you're dead inside a coffin. If I have to play dead, I told myself, I'm going to do it right. So I lay still, rigid, so rigid, my legs and arms began to ache, and I gritted my teeth as hard as I could. Then I felt a jolt, and I knew they were picking me up. And when they'd raised me in the air, I started laughing and couldn't stop. Maybe it's the same for the dead, I thought, who knows—maybe they wind up laughing, too.

I'D LOVE IT if you stayed for dinner, Viarengo told me later that afternoon. One by one the workers were leaving, a few by car, someone on a bike, someone on foot. As he said goodbye, Viarengo called each of them by name, his smile somewhat tender and somewhat of a grimace, for the sun. The last car pulled up next to him, and they chatted a bit. And when that last car was hurtling down the road, we kept on watching, until a long line of dust carried over the plains. That one over there's going out tomorrow at dawn, Viarengo said, pointing to a truck parked at an angle. The whole afternoon they'd loaded up the coffins, taken from those lying in the sun, passing them up steadily, never stopping, almost as if they weren't coffins at all, just one very long box. They're going to Germany, he said, staring at the truck. They're going to Germany, he said again, as he came over to where I was sitting, on a low wall.

You used to visit him every Sunday. Viarengo spoke slowly, a few words slipping out, then pausing, as though cut off by the wind. Meanwhile, the sun grew weaker, coloring the fields; the air grew still. You know, Viarengo said, I could always hear your mother before I ever saw her coming from down there. And to him, *down there* was the point where, shortly before, that car had been swallowed up, the point along the road where things suddenly were no longer visible, the same point where they started to appear, like submarines rising. So few cars pass by, he said, when someone does, you notice, especially on a Sunday. Sundays, it's quiet as can be, and he opened his arms to it all. You know, early on, he said, striking a match, lighting his cigarette, your mother would come out here with Anselmi. We used to see quite a bit of each other, the three of us. Anselmi and your mother were new here, they were trying to figure this place out. Viarengo leaned forward as he spoke, his elbows on his knees, his attention divided between his thoughts and the fields beyond, as if no matter what, he had to keep his eye on the horizon. His expression was frank, his eyes narrowing when he took a drag off his cigarette. He was straining to see so far into the distance, he seemed to be discussing a time he could no longer find. After a while he said, She was so happy with Anselmi, at first. Too bad things turned out the way they did. And he tossed his cigarette to the ground. Then he got to his feet, stood, hands on his hips. We were both staring off into the distance, with me not wanting to ask what happened to you and him standing there, not wanting to be at his knees for that explosive question.

He went into the building and returned with two cans of beer. Look at that, he said, pointing to the sun, soon it'll be underground, too. He opened a beer and passed it to me. For a little while we didn't speak, both of us on the low wall by the edge of one building, the sun lengthening our shadows and the cicadas coming out. So quiet, Viarengo said, and he said it as if the quiet was his as well. You smoke just like your mother, he said and gave a snorting laugh. I looked at him, keeping a straight face, not wanting to laugh myself, mouth in a straight line, but when he burst out laughing I was laughing, too. We should think about dinner—you must be hungry, he said, almost in a whisper. I shrugged, there was no rush, and then Viarengo said, If you want, why not spend the night—there's plenty of room. And so the night came on, and we stayed where we were on that low wall, the building behind us, the beer cans lining up at our feet. Viarengo's voice grew softer and softer. Around us, the fields had disappeared, and along with the fields, everything was swallowed up in darkness. Viarengo cleared his throat. Still, Monica seems like a nice girl. And I could tell he'd been ready with that comment for some time now, that it was the only response he could think of to the question I hadn't asked.

I FELL ASLEEP WEARING my shoes and clothes and your photographs. I woke at dawn, as the truck was leaving. The headlights hit the building, and the room where I'd been sleeping grew suddenly bright. It took me a moment to put everything together, the cot I lay on, the objects tossed in a pile, an old motorcycle leaning against the wall. Then the truck moved, and the light shifted and cut the room in two, a saber slice above my head. I went to the window: Viarengo was out there, shouting to the driver and turning a large, imaginary steering wheel, first to the right, then to the left, then shouting, Good job. It was only when I stepped outside that I realized he'd put me up in a shed or more likely, a garage, judging from the contents. But I'd drunk too much the night before to realize what was going on. All I remembered was the lightbulb swinging over the table when Viarengo hit it, and those photographs he pulled out sometime during dinner.

So you died alone, like a sick dog that couldn't even lick herself clean, the other dogs no longer willing to come around. When Viarengo told me, over dinner the night before, he wanted to prepare me for the photos I was about to see and kept saying, You sure you want to see these? Then he set them there on the table for a long while, before taking them out. He left and returned through the doorway that was just a frame with a sheet of dirty, paint-spattered nylon hanging down. You let yourself rot, Viarengo explained, his hand on the box of photographs. You abused yourself, alcohol, God knows what. He clamped the lid down with his arm, as if to keep the wind shut inside, giving me time to brace myself. Then I saw you, and I burst out laughing—that couldn't be you. Viarengo cut me off, his eyes hard. In those photos, you were an exploded body, misshapen, your hair gray, glued to your skull, always with a cigarette between your fingers. You were walking, you were inside a cape that made you look even bigger, your entire body leading down to those still small feet, like a mattress trying to stuff itself into a pillowcase. In every photo, Christian was there, too, though unintentionally. Viarengo stepped out for a cigarette, not wanting to be in the middle of this, this encounter between you and me. The more I stared at you in those photos, the more I drank. Then I saw you in a closeup, the hair on your chin, you, who spent so much time in front of the mirror, plucking the last stray stub from your eyebrows. When Viarengo returned, I said, Who took these? I did, he said, with no expression, out of expressions by now. There, he added, pointing outside. She hardly let anyone see her anymore—I was one of the few. I gathered the photos in a pile and started going through them again, one after the other. When you showed up again with that fuzz on your chin, I ran outside. Just in time to get out the door, lean against the wall, and throw up.

And what happened after that, I can't recall, just me waking to headlights, that truck leaving for Germany loaded with caskets for the dead, and your photos spread over me like a blanket. When he saw me outside, Viarengo grinned and shouted, Good morning, Lorenzo. I waved and sat down on the low wall; I stared out over the fields beginning to take shape. My head ached from beer and lack of sleep, and Viarengo kept shouting instructions at the truck, the driver hitting the horn by accident with his arm. I went back inside and gathered up the few things I'd brought and slipped them into my backpack, along with the photographs. Seeing it now, that shed was definitely a garage. The motorcycle leaned up against the wall had flat tires and a dusty seat. Next to the motorcycle was a metal cabinet with boxes of screws, bolts, and pliers; an old iron sat on a shelf, along with an electric radiator, an older model, long out of use. I heard the truck drive off, the slow shifting of gears, the noise gradually weakening. When I stepped back outside, I told Viarengo, I'm going to head out. Where to, he said, you're on foot. Let's have some coffee, and then I'll give you a lift. So we sat down where we'd had our supper, the table still uncleared. And this wasn't much different from the shed, either, the crusty floor, tools lying around. I have some of your mother's boxes, he said, maybe you'll want them. It was five in the morning, and he was already wearing his baseball cap. Don't you ever take it off? He smiled like he'd been waiting for that question. The day begins when you put on your hat, he said, and it ends when you take it off.

O NE DAY YOU even had me try out the egg. You took me to the factory on a Sunday morning, it was raining, and we told Dad we were only going for a stroll downtown. We were like thieves breaking into the building, even though it was yours. While you turned the key, you kept looking around, and I could feel my heart beating under my wet sweater. We shut the door behind us and ran, me clutching your hand and you with your heels tick-ticking, tracking our crime. You'd promised me that egg, a promise that had swelled to such proportions, I'd been afraid to even hold you to it. We were inside, and the building was empty, the offices, empty, and the coatracks were like skeletons lurking in the lobby. And that silence—in a place where you normally had to scream. More than silence—an emptiness that made it hard to breathe, as if they'd sucked out all the noise, and with it, all the air.

When we reached the egg room, you cracked the door open and poked your head inside. I stayed back a bit; from out here, the egg looked like a beached whale. Then you opened the door and we stepped into the room. Just me, you, and the egg. You started pushing buttons, raising and lowering levers, and the egg began to beep, and a ring of colored lights was blinking, and then everything subsided, and the egg went dormant. You walked over, told me, Take off your clothes and come get in, and I stared at you, terrified, like my first time in the pool. You'll see—it's fun, you said, everyone who's done it says so. I dropped my pants around my ankles and stepped out of them. You helped me with my sweater, pulling it off from above, me with my arms up, eyes closed, and then came my shirt and undershirt. You told me to climb the step, and you said, Usually fat people go in here—you're the exception. So I lay down inside; there was plenty of room, comfortable padding, and a velvety-soft headrest. You said goodbye as you shut the egg, and I was frightened again, No, wait, I tried to say, but the lid came down and swallowed up my words. Inside, the light was dim; I saw myself from above, in a mirror, and I wondered if dead people had a mirror, too, in their casket. I lay still; I couldn't hear a thing, not outside, not inside, only heat and the sensation of evaporating, exhaling.

When the egg opened, you were standing next to your partner, both of you laughing at the look on my face. I wasn't expecting your partner, to see him there, the two of you laughing, and me in my underwear, my face all sweaty, my hair mashed down on my forehead. I glared at you and didn't say anything, but I hated you with a passion—if I weren't in my underwear, stuck inside that egg, I would have ripped out your eyes and your hair. While you were getting me out, you said, I didn't realize, and I knew you were talking about him, and you looked amused and embarrassed at the same time. Your partner was making fun of me, of my underwear, my hair, how girly I was. You were helping me get dressed and also laughing at what he was saying, but then you'd turn and tell him, Come on—quit it—can't you see he's upset? And your partner would say, Sure, sure, but soon was right back at it again.

Then you took me to the bar, and I was hoping we'd be rid of him, but there he was, sitting at a small table. It wasn't the first time—these Sunday encounters that you always pretended were a surprise. You never know, you'd say, but over the years, I did know where we'd be going when we got dressed up on a Sunday morning. You in front of the mirror, staring at yourself, running your hands over your hips, checking the fit of your clothes. At the bar, the two of you drinking red wine, smoking your cigarettes. He spoke quietly but threw open his mouth when he laughed; he'd slip his hand between your legs, pretend it was a joke, tell me, You're not getting jealous, are you? You, pretending to put off his offensives, Quit it, you'd say. That Sunday, your partner asked me if I liked little girls, and he grinned. You gave him a playful slap. Stop it, I said, practically screaming in his face, but he'd already reached between my legs, was squeezing, hurting me. And the two of you were laughing and kissing, after three glasses of wine, you didn't want to and kept saying, Leave me alone, and him grabbing your head, your tongues in each other's mouths.

In the car, I refused to speak, and you kept trying to make me laugh and until you did, we wouldn't go home. When I finally laughed, you'd kiss me, and you didn't even have to tell me not to say a word of this to Dad.

I N THE BEGINNING, you often called from Romania, then less and less. These were your early trips, two weeks there and back at most. The telephone would ring late at night, with me already in bed and Dad in his easy chair in front of the TV. When he carried me to bed, I tried to come up with any excuse at all to wait just a little bit longer. I gave lengthy, articulate speeches, talking fast, words running together, pronounced so quickly, they got caught in my teeth. I was so agitated as I spoke, I could feel the sweat running down my hair and inside my pajamas. Every word I spoke felt like a bulwark against sleep, a few more captured meters in the direction of your phone call. Then Dad would get up from his chair and tell me negotiation time was through. He'd come toward me, not speaking, taking in all my contempt, my eyes saying, You don't matter, letting me hit him, the same way you'd flail at his chest, while he waited, nothing more, until you were done. Sometimes he'd swing me over his shoulder like a dying person, a sack of seed, and carry me off to bed. He was trying to be playful, but this way he could also avoid my eyes. While I just felt I was being kidnapped by the worst criminal there was.

The telephone rang later and later. As soon as Dad closed my door, I'd sit up against the headboard, knees to my chest, trying to stay awake. When I heard the phone, I'd leap out of bed and into the hall, and race up the stairs. Dad would be in his easy chair talking softly with you, maybe not to wake me, maybe only because it was nighttime and you were speaking softly on the other end. And you only asked me questions, about school, my homework, Dad, and my answers were always the same, because I was the one who was still at home leading the same life as before; you were the one who'd left, who'd changed everything. To my questions, all you answered was Don't worry, baby, everything's fine. So when our phone calls ended, I knew nothing about you, but I was happy all the same: telling you things was enough. I'd hand the phone back to Dad, and every time he'd say, Lula, but you'd already hung up. And then you started staying away longer and calling less and less, with me falling asleep against the headboard and Dad in his easy chair in the living room with the television on. Sometimes I'd hear him come into my room in the middle of the night, and he'd pull me out of my crouch, and quietly settle me under the covers. Then he'd shut the door again and I'd hear his bed hit the wall when he climbed in. And both of us would sleep like it was just a night, like any other night.

In the morning, we'd look at each other and Dad would say, You know it's not that easy to get through. The two of us would be on our stools at the kitchen counter, with our mugs and the metal tin of cookies. It was the same thing for lunch, and after lunch, dinner, the two of us not talking, as though silence was our only shared language. Saturday afternoons we'd go for a bike ride, him in front, blocking the wind, and me behind, following, not asking anything, not calling to him, not saying a word. When we got home, he'd do the same thing as you, make me bread and chocolate and set me on the couch with a blanket in front of the TV. He'd sit down beside me, in your usual spot. And I could tell how awkward he was, tender and embarrassed at the same time. And we kept waiting for you to come home, and you kept putting it off. Waiting, for both of us, was the only condition that justified our being together in the same house.

I left you notes on your nightstand, when you were away. I didn't know when you'd arrive, if you'd arrive when I wasn't home: I wanted you to see my greeting. So I'd sneak into your bedroom when Dad wasn't looking and leave you a note. I'd slip it under the alarm clock—

we both knew that was our secret place. I wrote, Hi, Mommy, or just a few things that had happened, that I didn't want to say over the phone. That the neighbors' dog had run away, for instance; I wrote this down in a little note and left it under the alarm clock. I wrote, Welcome back, Mommy, I'm really glad you're home. Three days ago the neighbors' dog ran away everyone is worried. Then I'd come home, and you weren't back. The next morning, I wrote another note, changing the number of days since the neighbors' dog ran away. Welcome back, Mommy, I'm really glad you're home. Four days ago the neighbors' dog ran away everyone is worried. Welcome back, Mommy, I'm really glad you're home. Five days ago the neighbors' dog ran away everyone is worried. Welcome back, Mommy, I'm really glad you're home. Thirty-four days ago the neighbors' dog ran away everyone is worried. When you truly, finally came back, it was seventy-six days later, and there was a column of scratched-out numbers, the corrected number on top. And the neighbors' dog had already come home.

I SAW CHRISTIAN outside your building, sitting on the steps, staring at his feet. Viarengo and I pulled up, and he raised his head and suddenly sat up, like he'd been caught sleeping on duty. I said, I would've called, and he answered, I was here, like he'd been there forever. Viarengo came toward Christian, ready to hug him, arms wide, chest out. And Christian had no other choice but to be hugged. Viarengo pounded him on the back a few more times, almost surprised to find him safe and sound. Then he took Christian's face between his hands and shouted, Hello, laughing, and for the first time, I saw Christian blush and look his age. He started laughing, too, showing his crooked teeth, and stepping out of that hug, embarrassed. You're never around, Viarengo said, but I love you anyway. You're not too bad, you Romanians. They're not too bad at all, he told me, pointing at Christian.

We pulled your boxes from the car, one after the other, and carried them to the elevator as if they were a parcel of goods, no questions allowed, don't ask, don't even try. We propped the front door open with a box, to free up our movements. Everything unloaded, Viarengo said, I better get going—it's late. So we leaned against the hood of the car and had a cigarette, Viarengo constantly adjusting his cap. Living so far out, he said, I don't like the city anymore. Ten years I've been here, he added, and now Bucharest is as ugly as us. Christian glanced at me, and said, That's not true. Fifteen years ago, he said, it was the Middle Ages here. And I remembered you, fifteen years ago, saying, It's the future there, and apparently the future *was* there, right smack in the Middle Ages. I'll come up, too, Viarengo said, springing away from the car. I only saw that apartment before your mother moved in.

We loaded the boxes onto the elevator; there was no room for us. Viarengo told me, Squeeze on in—climb up, so I scrambled up and sat on a box with my legs hanging down. It felt like I was bringing you your things by carriage, me on the box seat, the whole load behind me. I said, Once I'm up, I'll send the elevator back down. All seven floors, I breathed slowly, the elevator scraping the wall at every floor. Then it jolted to a stop, the doors opened, and there in front of me was your door. Me on my box, and you on the other side, not more than a meter away. I jumped down and started unloading the boxes and piling them by your door. Then I sent the elevator down and I took a seat on the mat, my back against the door. Like I used to do sometimes, with you. I'd say, I'm leaving, then I'd go out and sit down on the doormat. You knew and after a little while you'd shout at me from inside, Come on—let's kiss and make up, and I'd get to my feet, grip the doorknob, and step inside. You'd be the same as when I left you, and you'd barely look up to see me wriggling my way back in.

It was Christian who let us into your apartment; he signaled for us to wait while he deactivated the alarm, then, like a realtor, he said, Please. He and Viarengo stepped aside. And I found myself nodding, saying, Well, this is it, and in unison, they said, Yeah. And all I could think, standing inside this ordinary apartment, was that I didn't know it, I didn't know your home. That smell hitting me was a smell I had nothing to do with, the smell of you. I started walking around, a stark living room, yellowing walls, bookshelves with hardly any books. Christian and Viarengo stayed back, with me touching everything I saw, running my hand along tables, picking up knick-knacks. I walked over to the window, pulled back the curtains, and looked for my hotel window. Christian came forward, stretched out his arm. It's that one, he said. Then he opened the window and the noise of Bucharest blew in like a gust of wind, and with it, church bells. I thanked him; I'd felt like I was in a vacuum. Next to the window hung a photo of me, from years before. You're just the same, Christian said. I could tell he was forcing himself not to whisper. Then he took me to your bedroom, a double bed and a single nightstand against a wall. We stood in your room a while, not speaking, and we stared at that bed, as if you were still there. Viarengo came in as well and stood beside me; he put his hand on my shoulder. Then he stared at the bed, as if you were still there, and he took off his cap.

WE SAW THEM slip past, one after the other, the snouts of their cars. Christian and I were sitting in the square, each with a beer, a small table between us. They went by, all of them the same, first the hoods of those enormous SUVs, then the elbow out the window, and finally the sunglasses perched on a nose. All of them going by, staring, slowing down, smiling wider, then continuing on a few more meters. They were driving around the square, then coming to sit at the tables. Once in a while, Christian greeted someone, raised a hand or an eyebrow. Italians, he said, motioning to the line of cars. And at one point, there, poking out from one of those windows, was Anselmi's elbow. He stopped beside us, raised his sunglasses to give me a wink, then dropped them back on his nose and drove on in his convoy. Christian acknowledged him with a lift of his chin, not looking him in the eye, and turned back again toward the square.

Soon Anselmi was sitting beside us with five other men, all of them saying hello to me when they sat down. We took up two tables in that patio area growing steadily more crowded, people coming in waves, nearly all of them girls and men like Anselmi. So you decided to stay? he asked, alluding to the girls yet again, with a wink. A few more days, I answered, but he was no longer listening, tossing out greetings in every direction. That's smart, he told me, when my answer reached his brain. Then he introduced his friends; we shook hands and feigned getting up, just reaching across the tables. We're all pioneers, Anselmi said, summing up our handshakes. Here's to the pioneers, he said, and raised his beer, gesturing for the others to toast as well. The others answered by simply lifting their glasses, and Christian and I, not thinking, did the same. One of them makes furniture, Christian whispered to me, leaning close. And those others—one's in insurance, another shoes, and the other two, I couldn't say.

Do you see? Anselmi was elbowing me in the stomach, making sure I noticed all the girls at the other tables. You see how they're looking at us? He was waving to them as he spoke, and they waved back. They know right away who's got money, he said. Look at them, he whispered, meaning his five friends. Look how ugly they are. But here, they could start over. In Italy, they didn't mean shit. And now—he was shouting a little—now, here they are. This last part he said as if someone had just taken a sword and hacked a box in two and out stepped his friends, unscathed. And after he said this, his friends looked even flabbier, and I couldn't help staring at their double chins, their hairy nostrils, their sweaty, bald heads, their sausage fingers. But I could also see the intensity in their eyes, the intensity of men starting over. Christian didn't say a word. And other Italians kept arriving, staying a short while, then leaving again. Almost before I knew it, the girls at the next table over were now sitting at ours. Anselmi bought drinks, the other men offered cigarettes, and the girls were drinking, smoking, and laughing a great deal. Anselmi introduced them to me, couldn't remember their names, kept saying, You like them?, and to the girls, laughing, He's the best-looking of the bunch—and the youngest. Guys like him, he said, pointing at Christian, you already know about them, don't you? You ask me, you seen one Romanian, you seen 'em all. No—just kidding. This guy, he works with me, he said, and slapped Christian on the thigh. The girls laughed and exchanged a few words in Romanian with Christian, as if to say, You're harmless.

We left them at the table with handshakes all around. Before we left, Anselmi told me, We need to talk, and I said I agreed. He sat down again, looking pensive for a moment, then went back to waving his hands in the air. Christian lit a cigarette and said, What a piece of shit. He said this with no Romanian inflection, clearly, like he'd been sitting on it for days, had wanted to say it for a while, but only felt ready now. Yeah, I said, and finally, I knew he trusted me. You know what I think, I told him, walking up to Anselmi's car. I pulled the set of keys from my pocket, tucked one between my finger and thumb, came closer, and dragged that key all along the side panel, from the rear-end to the hood. Christian pulled out a bunch of keys as well, and he walked along the other side, doing the same. Then we looked at each other, not saying a word, and took off running.

CHRISTIAN SAID, YOU can even see it from the moon, with a jerk of his chin toward the Ceauşescu Palace. And it was suddenly there, erupting between two buildings. Christian seemed to be on the lookout for it, kept spotting it as we walked around the city. He'd raise his arm, while I came close and looked down his arm to his pointing finger, and it was always there, the Ceauşescu Palace, though never complete. I'd nod, he'd lower his arm, and we'd go on until the next sighting. You can even see it from the moon, he said again and stopped, and he looked up, as though trying to find, up there in the sky, the exact point where someone else was looking down. So I looked up, too, and we stayed like that, focused on the sky, and a spot neither one of us could guess at. It's not like you can see just anything from the moon, he said, and he wore an expression of pride, for the visibility of the Ceauşescu Palace, but his face also showed disappointment, and this was much more private. As though, from the moon, the two of us couldn't be seen, so there was no use in raising your arms, no use screaming and waving hello.

He stopped, checked the time on his phone, and glanced at me out of the corner of his eye, with the look of someone who's just thought of breaking some rule. Then he said, You want to see it?, and I knew he was the one who wanted us to go. Is that allowed? I said. The Palace went on forever. We walked around three sides looking for the entrance, but it was like we never moved, each side, identical to the last. Then there was a long line of people, and Christian was clearing the way for me, asking for information, like he was my bodyguard. We bought our tickets, and they told us to wait, that the tour started in half an hour. So we joined all the others crowded into the lobby, cameras around their necks, Bermuda shorts, postcards of Bucharest, and a few vampires on backpacks and T-shirts, with sunk-in fangs. We're the only Italians, Christian said. Mostly, those around us were British or German, and Ceauşescu's name kept coming up, everyone looking around like he might pop out at any second.

The entire tour, Christian stuck close to the guide, wanting to hear every word, in spite of not knowing much English. We all moved on command, whenever the guide said, *Follow me, please*. Whenever she said, *Follow me*, we started whispering, as one by one we stepped out from the silence where we'd been listening. Then, slowly, we'd set off again, the guide in front, Christian and I right behind, and after us came all the others. And so we passed through vast rooms, sumptuous corridors, the guide providing a wealth of numbers about the tons of marble, all the fine crystal, the dimensions, and the space's current use. When she'd finished her catalog of materials and measurements, she said, *Follow me, please*, and moved on to the next room, just as sumptuous, just as vast, and with tons of marble and fine crystal comparable to what came before. In less than a half hour, we were standing outside again by the entranceway, all of us, our faces furrowed with disappointment. The guide had walked us through only one floor, and then we had to leave. But worst of all, she never mentioned Ceaușescu. Not even once. We'd gone in there to learn about him, what he'd been capable of, but instead he was the emptiness the guide talked around, in her composed speech on tonnage, meters, numbers. As though decency had come between pain and pride, as though evil could be displayed, as long as it was never mentioned, not even once.

And so we left, Christian, with sagging shoulders, staring at the ground. Sorry, he said. I laid my hand on the nape of his neck and told him not to worry. He looked at me and shook his head slightly, so I'd understand that he wasn't disappointed about all of it. I saw anger in his eyes, loaded, ready to fire. He said, They're ashamed. Ashamed of what? I asked. He stopped in the middle of the street. He looked at me, then the Palace. Then he said, They're ashamed to be proud of it.

THEY TOOK ME for a thief, the people in your building. They all came out together, someone running down from the eighth floor, someone at the railing, the only door on your floor still closed had someone at the peephole. They found me there, your door open, my bag in my hand and the alarm howling up and down the stairs. We all stared at each other a moment, not speaking, all of them focused on my face, and me looking each of them over in turn. One little old lady stepped out from the group and came toward me, pushed me aside, waving me off, and she walked in, typed in the code on the panel, and the alarm stopped howling. Then she walked back out and squeezed in among the others crammed onto the landing and joined them in glaring at me. I broke the silence with a single word, Fiu, while tapping myself on the chest. One of the few Romanian words I knew, that I'd learned from Christian. So all I said was, Fiu, Son, and there was a widespread sigh, and one after the other, they walked away. Before going, the lady who'd turned off the alarm came forward holding a sheet of paper with numbers on it, the alarm code, which I'd copied down wrong. And only then did I realize the code was my birthday.

And so the door closed, and you and I were left in a silence that felt like it must have come searching for you. I walked softly, not to be heard, almost. There was a time we would play this game, would search for each other around the house, with me always hiding under the bed, and you in the tub. And when you found me, you grabbed hold of my feet and pulled me out like a dresser drawer. One by one, I tried every chair, sat down, gazed at the room. In every chair I let my weight down slowly, not wanting to make too much noise, unseemly creaking. And after the chairs, the couch, the recliner; then I opened drawers, pulled out a fork and knife and wondered how you could eat with them, so heavy, so oxidized, so cold to the touch. I set myself a place, there was no tablecloth, just two placemats; I took a plate left to dry by the sink and the overturned glass beside it, a white water ring on steel. I changed my seat, then sat down on each side of the table, trying to imagine which was yours. Another game we used to play—I'd turn around, you'd briefly take a seat, and I had to guess. I'd sit down, contemplate, you'd tell me to close my eyes and search for warmth, your shape. I almost always managed it; I'd open my eyes, look at you and say, You were here, and you'd say, You're the greatest magician I know. Now, in your apartment on the seventh floor, I did the same thing, searching for you on your kitchen chairs, trying to guess where you were. But I didn't know what to search for anymore, after all this time, what heat to go hunting for, what shape you'd taken in the meantime. And so I sat down on each one, and after the first round, a second, a third, a fourth, and the only heat I found was mine, the only shape was mine, my legs, my seat on the chair.

The apartment had grown dark now, but I barely noticed, sitting in the kitchen before an empty plate. I went into the bathroom, got undressed, stepped into the shower: you're only home after your first shower. I washed with your sliver of soap, dried myself with your bathrobe, brushed my teeth with your toothbrush, still on the sink, like an old flag on an abandoned fortress. I scraped it over my teeth, rooting around in my mouth, between my tongue and palate, and then I set it back, upright, with its unruly bristles. The mirror was too low—it cut off my head—and to think there was a time you used to lift me up, to look into my eyes. I was still wet when I left the bathroom, a trail of droplets behind me. I turned off all the lights, except the nightstand lamp. I took my pajamas from my bag, put them on, and went over to your bed. I dropped onto it, tried to bounce, then slipped under the covers. And it was almost as if I felt your bones, under there, that I was lying between bone and muscle and had to stay very still, or else I'd hurt you.

WE WOUND UP next to each other, towel around our shoulders, neck back, and a young woman behind each of us, preparing to cup our head in her hands. Anselmi had called at eight, your phone ringing, and I stared at it bitterly, as though it had no right to ring, without you there. But I stayed at the table, just let it ring until it stopped, and the kitchen went back to being quiet. I finished my coffee while I stared outside; you'd left enough in the can for one morning coffee, maybe two. Then the telephone started ringing again, I turned and looked and let it die. I washed the espresso cup and set it dripping by the sink, next to your glass and plate. And when the phone began to ring again, I walked over and picked up the receiver. I put it to my ear and for a moment, didn't speak. Then I said, Hello, and I randomly thought of the first time you'd answered the phone with a Romanian Alo, and I'd slammed the phone down, thinking I'd wound up in someone else's home. So I added an Alo to my Hello, and Anselmi, on the other end, shouted, What're you—Romanian now? Then he said, Meet me at the barber's, and hung up.

Anselmi was whimpering with pleasure before they even started; I heard the girl behind me testing the temperature on her own skin, before she started washing my hair, a kindness I wouldn't expect from a stranger. Then we both had our heads under the water, shampoo, massages, fingers slipping behind our ears, partly washing, partly as little walls, making sure only our hair got wet. Anselmi acted as though everything in the place was his, the sink, shampoo, towel, entire staff. The girl standing behind him treated him almost fondly, maybe because of their situation, with him having to behave himself, his neck caught in a fissure while he stared up at the ceiling. So how you doing in that apartment? he asked. Fine, thanks, I said, staring up at the ceiling myself, as though question and response might converge up there. It's really quiet in that apartment, he said. Then he asked me how long I was planning on staying, and I said, I don't know yet, and he said, Sure, sure, of course, almost with a sense of decorum. Then the girls finished our shampoos, wrapped our heads in towels, had us sit up. And so we looked at each other, under our turbans, and Anselmi said, Here we are, as if our exchange was still up there, stuck on the ceiling.

Same cut for both of us, Anselmi told the two girls; they nodded, and raised our styling chairs by pumping a pedal, as though inflating a rubber raft. When the girl working on me started combing my hair I said, Actually, I'd like it really short, and she answered, My pleasure. Then looking at himself in the mirror, Anselmi said, I want to tell you about your mother, and looking straight into my own eyes, I said, Of course you do. He started with, You know how these things work—No, I said, and that was all. Your mother was an exceptional woman, he started again, trying a different tack. He was quiet then, and I could tell he wasn't trying to think of what he might say—he was just adjusting his expression, to avoid looking bored. You don't know what to say, I told him, swinging around, breaking off our mirror mediation. No, he answered. He paused, nervously brushed away the girl's hand with the scissors. Actually, no, he said. Of course not, I said, sitting up in my chair. The girls were silent, somewhat frightened, focusing on their work. I watched my hair, bit by bit, dropping onto the white towel, like wet leaves on snow. Every now and then, the girl asked if she should stop and I'd say, A little more, please, and she'd say, My pleasure. After that No, Anselmi had nothing more to say, not to me, not to the girl giving him his regular haircut.

How'd she die? I asked him when we left. Anselmi lit a cigarette and started walking. How'd she die? he said, like everybody dies—boom. As if you had blown up. Her heart, he said. Her heart stopped. He turned to me, She let herself die. He looked at me as if he were challenging me with the truth, as if he wanted to fling your corpse down on top of me. I don't understand, I said, grabbing hold of his arm. There's nothing to understand, he said, jerking away. She let herself rot—she destroyed herself, day after day. Do you have any idea how much she stank, he said, because she wouldn't bathe? He curled his lip. Do you have any idea how much she drank?—how disgusting a rotting woman can be? No, I said. And you have no idea what it was like to find her, dead for days, swollen, to be called in by the neighbors. No—you have no idea, kid—because you're just a kid. We stared at each other, people walking past, someone turned, looked back toward the street. And you—where were you? I screamed in his face. He stared at the ground, then up at me. He poked me in the chest. And where were you? he said.

I stood frozen, Anselmi walking off, leaving me with that question. I could still feel his finger. I watched him walk away, like someone who knew he was being watched, his every move intentional. So you'd frightened him, finding you there, your neighbors, who could smell you from under the door, that smell spreading through the entire floor, down the stairs. They probably kept exchanging looks, for days, not knowing what to do, they probably knocked, rang the bell. Then

someone must have called, and Anselmi, arriving in his sunglasses,
opening your door with his keys, then hands over his nose, turning,
looking at the neighbors crowded into your doorway.

You'd also try to make a turkey, and every time, it wound up burnt in the oven. You'd come home from your trips and say, Tonight I'm making you a gigantic turkey, then you'd look at Dad and correct yourself, I'm making the two of you a gigantic turkey. The longer you were away, the more you'd come back and set yourself at the stove, saying, Away with you both, out of my kingdom, let me work. But then you didn't know where things were; I could hear you opening cupboards, closing drawers, swearing up a storm, dropping things. Until Dad walked into the kitchen, always right before you called, as if by chance. When he left it was far quieter; you'd start singing, open the valves, turn on the gas. Dad would pass me and wink, our agreement to keep you happy. You constantly came out of the kitchen, wandering around the house in your apron, just so we'd see. Then you went back to the stove and fussed with the pots and the wooden forks, partly playing with the saucepans, partly playing at being a wife and mother.

In the beginning, the turkey was for fancy occasions, then it was for your homecomings, more and more infrequent. We'd go buy it together, you saying, I'd like a nice, big turkey and the butcher telling you, Look at this beauty, holding the bird up like an infant. Then he'd wrap it in paper, and we'd take it home in a shopping bag, and I sensed it, crouching in the dark, like an illegal alien hiding in the back of a truck. At home you'd pull it out of the bag, tear off the paper, and slam it down naked on the marble tabletop, and then you'd pull out the guts, disgusted, face turned away. You'd make me look at the guts in your hand, saying, Here's what we have inside, and I'd say, I'm no turkey, and then I'd run into the other room. And every time, you'd say, Never again, about the turkey, that it took too much effort, was violent, disgusting. But then you'd go away for a long time, and the turkey would be back for further torture on our kitchen table.

Those nights you made a turkey you'd say, I want you to keep an eye on it and make sure it doesn't escape. You'd say, There's no trusting an animal like that. And you'd turn on the oven light, and I'd peer in, through the glass, and see it, immobile, not going anywhere. I'd squat down in front of it, arms crossed over my knees, my rear practically hitting the floor. We'd stay like that, facing off, lazily playing our roles, me as guard, turkey as sacrificial victim. You'd come in now and then and lay your hand on my head and say, How's our turkey doing? I'd turn, my head rotating under your hand, and say, Asleep but sweating. What was clear, though: that turkey had no intention of flying the coop. Then you'd leave and I'd stay, and the heat emanating from the oven seemed like the turkey's way of communicating with me. To see it, you'd think it had nothing to say, but then there was that heat coming out, the language of a turkey locked inside an oven.

And then it always seemed like something happened, and the turkey would burn. I'd get fed up after a while, watching it sweating in there. I'd start sweating myself, and peel off my sweater, then my shirt, and then I couldn't stand it anymore. So I'd go to my room and play; you stopped checking on the turkey in the oven, and in the oven, the turkey would cook for far too long. From my room I'd hear you screaming—at first you sounded amused, then angrier and angrier, until you were furious. And I knew it had happened again—burnt turkey. The last few times, when it happened, you'd throw things on the floor, pound the fridge, even start crying. At first Dad would come to the rescue, when you were crying, but when it was clear you'd come home only to get ready to leave again, he didn't come in anymore to let you cry in his arms. He'd stand by the living-room window, and I'd see him there, and I wasn't sure what I should do. Once I ran into the kitchen and found you sitting on the floor, back against the fridge, and you pointed to the charred turkey, the oven wide open, heat pouring out.

Roasted or burned, though, the turkey always went on the table. And the more burned it was, the more it seemed like an act of defiance. You'd slap it on our plates, just as it was. And we ate that turkey, the three of us, heads down, not peeling off the blackened skin, not looking each other in the eye.

D AD STOPPED TAKING you to the airport one rainy Monday. Before that, we all went together: Dad would start the car in the driveway and leave it running and wait for us. He'd load your bags, clean the car windows, remove any stray paper on the seats. You and I would always come out late, you with all the things you kept forgetting, just at the door, and me right behind you, almost following in your footsteps. Dad would wait by the car that all the while was just sitting there, getting hotter. When we were finally out the door, the two of us, we were always running, and due to the flurry of forgotten things, our hope of leaving early always turned into leaving late. So Dad would open the door, you'd shout, Oh god, I'm going to miss my flight, and I'd slide down, so we could go faster. At the airport, we'd just manage to get there in time, you and I would get out at Departures, and Dad would go park. We always checked in together, me with one of your suit-cases, like I was coming along. And every time, we played our weight game; first the lady weighed your bags, and then you said, Here's the last one. All the check-in ladies would start laughing when you said this, and they'd make me get on the scale and tell me how much I weighed as a suitcase. Then you'd say, Get down now, so you don't wind up in the plane's tummy, and I'd jump down as the other bags were being carried away on the conveyer belt. The last time I'd see you would be at security; you always made the detector go off, and the officers would take you aside. In the beginning, I'd look at Dad when the officers approached you, but he'd just lay his warm hand on my head. While you talked with them, you'd look at me, from the other side, and you'd start laughing, and I'd start laughing, too.

Then Dad stopped taking you to the airport. The night before he stopped, your partner came over; it was late when he rang the bell, and soon after I was shut inside my room. I brought my toys closer to the door, to hear what everyone was saying at that time of night. But it was pouring out, rain pounding on the windows, and what you were saying was swallowed up in thunder. So I couldn't understand much, mostly you and your partner talking, with Dad tossing out a blunt question now and then. At the sound of your voices, I imagined the three of you at the table, that these angry tones wouldn't be used on the couch and easy chair. Then for the first time, I heard Dad shouting, his voice slowly rising, as if the room were filling, breath by breath, with a hatred I'd never heard from him before. His voice kept swelling and I thought it might never stop, it was stifling, pressing against the walls, then the door to my room. I was sitting with my back against the door, and it felt like I had to push hard, to hold back that fury, to avoid having everything in the house burst wide open, hatred and turmoil whirling to a gale-force wind. I could hear you quietly repeating Dad's name over and over, but sounding unconvinced yourself, as though you'd been expecting that fury for some time. Your partner didn't seem to be there anymore, maybe Dad's shouting had swept him away, under the door. But then all that hatred disappeared, the wind suddenly died, and the walls and doors came down again like sails in the calm. And so the rain was pounding on the windows again, and the front door closed and carried your partner away.

Monday morning you had to leave. When I came into the kitchen, Dad was having his breakfast and you were running late, shoving your last forgotten things into your suitcase. In spite of last night's turmoil, the living room was tidy. I thought it would be a wreck, books on the floor, curtains pulled down, lying over the furniture, but it was just the same as before your partner had rung the doorbell, and you'd taken me by the hand, opened my bedroom door, turned on the light, and shoved me inside. I looked at Dad, and I knew we wouldn't be taking you to the airport that morning. Normally, Dad would already be outside, standing by the running car, waiting for us. Now he was there in the kitchen, looking someplace else. You said, Want to come with me in the taxi?, and I said, Sure, before you could finish. So we found ourselves sitting in the taxi, both of us in the back, while the driver went in to get your bags. You asked if I'd heard anything last night, and I kept my face blank, ready with a yes or no, depending on how much you wanted to tell me. You said, I know you heard, and then I nodded and looked down. I don't love Dad, you told me, breathing out in one long sigh as if it frightened you to say this, and when you couldn't breathe out anymore, I knew you weren't going to talk about your partner. And Dad? I asked, and you said, Now Dad knows. Then I asked, And me?, and you said, And you're here with me. In no time at all the airport was in view, the taxi pulled up to Departures, and the driver got out and left your bags on the sidewalk. We sat in the taxi a bit, just you and me, and before you got out, you said, No making that face now. Then you shut the door, handed the driver some money, and said, Take him home. You came up to my window and tapped your goodbye; you blew me a kiss, then you went through the revolving door. The taxi driver got back in the car, turned to me, and said, All right, young man, where to? But I knew I didn't have to tell him.

WE WERE ON either side of the street, both of us looking around to avoid looking at each other. Monica had slid a note under the door, an envelope with a note that read, Be at the Intercontinental, six o'clock. Written in Anselmi's peremptory style, with his arrogant bite. But the handwriting was rounded, girlish, balloons dotting the i's, and the name she signed at the bottom, *Mony*, also rounded, and pressed into the paper. And so here we were, me on one side of the street, her on the other, the Bucharest crossing signals counting down, rattling off numbers in reverse, as if something was always just about to begin. When the light reached zero, Monica waved me over, pointing to the car beside her, its hazards on. She said, Sorry, looking at the Dacia, then said, It's my dad's. We got in and drove off, and it felt like the first car you ever owned, a car so loud, we had to shout to be heard. It's charming, I told her, as the car coughed and sputtered off when the light changed. It's a piece of crap, she said, tugging on the gearshift, like she was yanking a stick away from a dog. I think it's charming, I said again, it reminds me of my mother's first car. In Romania? she asked, still struggling with the gearshift. No, in Italy. In Italy, she said, eyes on the road, they don't make such crappy cars.

Soon, almost before I knew it, we'd left Bucharest behind. Once outside the city, Monica said, You think it's so charming, you drive. And so I got behind the wheel of what, for me, was your first car, not Monica's father's car. And it was true—the only way to change gears was to tug on the gearshift, like yanking a stick away from a dog. Monica watched me and laughed. Still think it's charming? she asked when the Dacia stalled out in the middle of the road. Slightly less charming, I said, annoyed, the motor braying as I turned the key in vain. Soon two men were pushing us out of traffic, with tight, impatient expressions. At last the engine started, I saw the men in the rearview mirror slowing down, then stopping as we pulled out and waved our thanks out the windows. Charming, no? I said, now that it was over, and she answered, Very funny. However, yes. Very charming. Then she added, But it's still a piece of crap. Then, after a while, she said, We used to go on vacations, me, my mother and father. She looked over, to see my reaction, like this was almost a secret, that she'd had a life before all this, before all these colorful warehouses going by, before Anselmi. That she'd been a girl. When? I asked. A long time ago, she said, like centuries had passed, like she was well into old age, and not in her twenties. I used to go on vacation, too, I said, and I was back to thinking that the Dacia reminded me of your first car. And for a few moments, we were children together, Monica and I, the two of us in the back seat, listening to the voices of others from afar, drenched in the noise of the engine.

Monica started rummaging through the glovebox and other compartments, pulling out old keyrings, postcards, other things I couldn't see, my hands on the wheel. With each item she'd scream, No!, and laugh. In her zeal she squeezed between the front seats, slid into the back, the car wobbling and me laughing, saying, Careful—we might flip over. You know, the car's charming and all, but it's pretty beat up and might flip over. So she stayed in the back, stretched out on the seat, and told me about her vacations with her parents, to the mountains or the Black Sea, and about her hometown, in the middle of nowhere, that everyone had probably left by now. I couldn't see her in the rearview, only her legs when she raised them, pointing her toes at the ceiling. I kept going in the same direction; once in a while, I'd ask if we should stay on this road, and she'd say, Straight, straight. She talked about her little town nestled among the meadows, the blissful boredom of those summer days. Then she started singing; I could hear her behind me, through the noise. And I didn't say anything, just let her sing and poke her feet up, to show me she was still there. She suddenly stopped, sat up, and shifted behind me and said, I can't remember those songs now. When she said this, her voice sounded bright, surprised, like she'd just found money in her pocket. Then she screamed, No!, sounding even more shocked than those other times she'd screamed. My blanket! she shouted, laughing and clapping. We always used to stop, she said, we'd sit in a meadow, on my blanket. Then she said, Could we stop?, and I looked at her in the mirror and smiled. Where? I asked. Here, she said, pointing vaguely to the endless passing meadows. So we left the car and walked into the fields. And we lay down on the blanket, with it almost nightfall, and some lingering light in the sky. I lay with my hands clasped behind my neck. Why'd you want to see me? I asked. Monica rested her head on my chest. Because, she said, laughing, I wanted to tell you a few things I forgot.

I WATCHED HER WALK into the hotel, and then she didn't come back out. Anselmi had woken us that morning, Monica and I, lying on the blanket in the middle of the field, intertwined like laced fingers. I felt Monica's phone vibrating on my leg, and she took it from her pocket and clung to me for warmth. She opened her eyes, then, with the sun, she closed them again. She answered with Ello, not Hello, which I hadn't noticed before. It was Anselmi on the other end, screaming so loud, as usual, that I could hear him, too, in spite of the cars going by, the tractors in the fields, the planes flying over. Monica slipped her phone back in her pocket and sat up; she said, Good morning, as though we were in a private room, not a field, with trucks rumbling past just a few meters away. I said, Good morning, and sat up, too, and looked around. Where are we? I asked, and she said she didn't know. Anyway, we have to go, she said, and pushed herself up, getting to her feet. Is something wrong? I asked while she smoothed her hair, flicked grass off her sweater. I have some shit to take care of, she said, back to Anselmi's ugly language, but then she smiled at me with all her balloon-dotted i's. So I got up, too, and Monica gathered the blanket, folded it, and tucked it under her arm. Then she was suddenly pushing past me, laughing, and she raced toward the car, me in pursuit, trying to grab onto her sweater.

After she parked, Monica said, Wait here. Then she got out and went inside the hotel, and I saw her talking at the reception desk, her elbows on the counter. She didn't tell me anything about what she was doing, just I have some shit to take care of and Wait here. So I sat in her father's Dacia, only now, with her not there, I could smell the car, the strong odor of plaid shirts and leather-skinned men. After a while I got out, walked around the parking lot, the Bucharest cars going by, passing each other, honking in traffic. At last, Monica ran down the steps and waved for me to come. I followed her through the lobby and onto the elevator; we stopped on the sixth floor. She grabbed my arm and pulled me into a room, then shut the door and said, You have to help me. I sat down on the edge of the bed. We have to find a gold ring, she said. A wedding ring? I asked, and she nodded. Anselmi kept calling, wanting to know if the ring had shown up, if Monica had gone over the room completely. It's one of Anselmi's clients, she explained, and she rolled up the area rugs, and didn't talk for a while. You guys only come here for pussy, she said, and I immediately averted my eyes, not wanting to see her face when she talked this way, as she had the first time we met. Soon I was helping her look for a wedding ring, so Anselmi's client could avoid the embarrassment of facing some wife waiting for him at home. We pulled the covers off, flipped mattresses, slipped our hands down the toilet, emptied drawers, took the tiny bottles and snacks out of the mini-bar. Monica was searching furiously, and her panic was catching, the two of us panting in our T-shirts and Anselmi calling. In the end, we were on the floor, sweating, side by side, in a room that looked like it had been ransacked by a thief, or the police. Whoever it was, he'd taken that man's ring.

We wound up outside, on the hotel steps, Monica trying to explain things to Anselmi, one call after the other, until I finally grabbed her phone and turned it off. What are you doing? she asked, drawing back from me. Enough, I said. But he'll get really pissed, she said, and turned the phone back on. And he called again, and after it was over, Monica hurled her phone to the ground, and it shattered. I went to her where she knelt, crying, trying to put the pieces back together, and through her sobs she kept saying, God, why?, why?, no longer seeing me.

CHRISTIAN LET ME out at the warehouse. He pulled up and said, Give me a call, his foot on the clutch, his hand on the gearshift. He didn't turn to look at me, just stared straight ahead, through the windshield, stubbornly avoiding the warehouse to the right, out my window. Then he headed off, past the fields, in a cloud of dust and kicked-up gravel. The Italian flag and Juventus banner were still fluttering above; a lazy donkey was curled up, along the road. All around, just slanting evening shadows and the hum of cars that waned but never disappeared. Your name hanging like an oversight, the banner filling up when the wind decided. Then the gate jerked open, a metallic sound, the two wings opening, and a pickup slipping through, and onto the road. So all of a sudden I was standing right in front of the workers, who glanced at me, like I just happened to be passing by, out there in the countryside. Looking at me no differently than they would that donkey lying curled up at a distance. Then, just as they had opened, now the wings were swinging closed, and I jumped back to avoid being hit.

A small door opened in the middle of the gate, I hadn't noticed it before, and there stood Anselmi. I stepped through, ducking, and I was in the work yard. The door closed behind me with a thud. Everything was the same as the day I arrived, forklifts crossing from one side to the other, and workers taking smoke breaks in shifts, gloves in their back pocket. Anselmi grabbed my arm, and we walked into the building together, leaving the noise behind, enormous fans sweeping flies off the ceiling, the heat, the stench of accumulated sweat. The air conditioning's not working, Anselmi said. It was just like your firm in Italy, where you used to take me after school. The same furniture, same spaces, same lights, even the same mezzanine, like the one I used to dangle my feet over, while I waited. Except your parked car wasn't out there; our house wasn't out there; we weren't out there. Out there was another world, the one in the drawing, on the other side of the river, three hours by plane, twenty by car, thirty plus hours by bus. Out there was the place you used to talk about, a world where anything was possible. The Wild West. Anselmi was quiet, staring at me, proudly. Remind you of anything? he said, grinning. Of course, I said, looking away. We're still always us, he said with pride, and then, It's like a magic spell, in the same voice he might use with a child, as if I were still a child swinging my feet through the rails of a building exactly like this one. And it actually felt like the two of you had loaded that building onto a truck, hauled it away from Italy and plunked it down here, in the middle of the Romanian plains, in the heat, with Indians hiding in the bushes.

Anselmi's office was identical to the one where I used to do my homework, while you were walking up and down the lobby, employees sometimes beside you, talking to you, then turning and going back the way they came. Anselmi shut the door behind me, walked around the desk, took off his jacket, sat down in his office chair. I sat down across from him, my knees rubbing against the front of the desk. I tucked my hands under my legs while he gathered some papers together, stacked them loosely, then looked at me and said, Lorenzo. Behind me, I heard the door open; Anselmi gave a dismissive wave, and the door closed again. Lorenzo, he repeated, and I stared at him in silence. He studied his palms, Your mother, he said after a moment, she always held onto her shares—she never wanted to sell. Then he searched my face for a reaction. But I'm sure you already knew this, he said, goading, hinting at your monthly payments. Yeah, I said, I knew. Good, he said, looking at his hands again, I'd like to buy her shares. Let's make a deal. I pulled my hands out from under my thighs, let them hang now. Anselmi kept talking, but I'd stopped listening, just watched his moving lips, his hands waving, how he stared at his palms. So is it a deal? he said, and he came around the desk, laid a hand on my shoulder. I don't know, I said, and stood, shrugging off his hand. Anselmi stepped back. If you don't want to sell, he said, you can always work here—you already know the business.

After shaking his hand, I started to leave, and he said, Let me know. I closed the door behind me and went out onto the mezzanine; I leaned my elbows on the rail. Monica was going by below; she waved at me and smiled. I went down to the work yard, saw a forklift carrying a box with a drawing on the side of your weight-loss egg. From here, your machines heading out, to all parts of the world, to China, Russia, the Congo, for fat people to lose weight. I watched the forklift disappear inside the warehouse. Then I walked over to the door in the gate, and left. Christian sat smoking in his car, the window down. He saw me come out and started the engine. The donkey didn't budge.

THE WAY YOU left that last time, it was clear you wouldn't be coming back. Just hearing you say, I'll be back soon, your way to avoid explaining yourself, us hugging, talking. Dad had gone to work earlier than normal—he hadn't been taking you to the airport for a while. Your partner was out front, on the phone in his car, and he stayed in his car when he saw you come out with your suitcases. Did I get everything? you asked yourself, like you always did at the door, but this time you really meant everything. You stood there, one hand on the doorknob, one foot out, the rest of you inside. Then you said, I'll be back soon, and you blew me a kiss. I'm going to get you a gift, you added, that's beyond your wildest dreams. I didn't go to you, like I always did when you were leaving, running to you, partly a declaration of war, partly begging you to take me along. You said, I'll be back soon, and I knew I had to stay. So I stood beside the couch, watching you leave, and through the open door, I saw your partner's car. I stood there, not moving, a few meters from you, staring, like a dog that knows it has to stay home. And like a dog, I stared at that closed door, when you were no longer there.

Dad came back, with you gone a few hours and me on the couch, watching TV. He came in and walked through the rooms before even nodding hello. He wandered through the house, nervous, an expression in his eyes I'd never seen before: rage and fear. Maybe the same expression he'd had that night, when the house swelled with his hatred, when I pressed my back against the door, to keep it from bursting open. He wandered, furious, through the entire house, as if assuring himself you weren't hiding someplace. Then he came in and sat down beside me, and he laid his hand on my head and kept it there, while I kept staring at the television and tried to understand what was happening inside his hand. He picked up the remote and pushed the mute button. Then he turned to me; he squeezed my foot. He said, What're you watching?, and I shook my head, meaning, That's not the point. Do you understand what's happened? he asked, and I nodded, because that was the point. Then he turned toward the television, loosened his grip on my foot, and said, Your mother's gone. He said this helplessly, sounding almost drained, not angry anymore, not scared; he let go of my foot entirely. Your mother's gone, he said again, and this time, saying, Your mother, put an enormous distance between us. We sat like that, staring at the television set, both of us slouched back against the couch, people talking on the screen and us out there, not listening. We just sat next to each other, not saying a word, each of us with our own last name, and it suddenly felt foolish to be sitting on that couch like I was a son and he was my dad.

For days no one heard from you. Your mom even called—Hi, is your mom there, she said, this is your grandmother—and I thought it was a wrong number and hung up. Then you called, and it was two weeks later, and you kept saying, Sorry, sorry, but nothing more. I'm getting your gift ready, you said then, to counter my silence, but it'll take a little while. I heard your partner in the background, and he was talking to someone, too, both of you in the car, talking on your own. Below your voices, I could hear the road, because the Wild West, you'd told me, was full of roads and people rushing to arrive before the others. Sometimes I'd hear something louder, and you'd say, You know how the roads are over here, and I'd say, Yeah. Then we were cut off, and you didn't call back. When Dad came home, I told him you'd called and that you wanted to say hello. One day, a few weeks later, you asked to speak to him. Dad was outside clearing off the sidewalk, bagging leaves, something he did even before you went away. I set the receiver down on the table and went to the window; I waved, but he didn't see. So I came out and told him, Mom's on the phone. He slowly removed his gloves, staring at the window, as though you were inside. Now you, he said, handing me the broom, and then he disappeared through the door. I decided to sing while I swept, pretending I didn't want to hear what you two were saying. It was the first time you'd told me, Get Emilio, not Get Dad. So out of nowhere, he'd become my father, and now, out of nowhere, he no longer was. And when he came back outside, the phone call over, he was also Emilio to me.

ONTH AFTER MONTH you kept reminding me about your gift; years later, you gave it to me. That first year went by with a phone call every Sunday evening. I spoke to you while surrounded by your presents, the phone line leading down the hall, under my closed door, to me. I'd sit by the window, Dad outside my room, teasing me now and then, the phone sometimes sliding closer to the door. I'd see this and throw myself onto it like a rugby player. I was glad he was outside the door, that I didn't have to see his face when he tried to play with me, because he wasn't very good at it. Playing with me was something he forced himself to do, trying to take your place, and I forced myself to let him and hoped it would be over soon. You always called at eight o'clock on Sunday; you'd say, Did you know it's nine o'clock here?, and I'd say, That can't be. You'd say, What time is it?, and I'd look at the clock and say, Eight, and you'd say, You know how Mommy is—she lives in the future. How you were I learned over time. There came a point when you started skipping those Sunday phone calls, and then they were monthly. And I didn't need to get ready for them anymore, either, trailing the phone chord down the hall, under my door, and sitting surrounded by your presents. The phone would ring, and I'd just answer in the hall or the kitchen, and sometimes it was you on the other end, but mostly, someone else.

One day on the phone you said, Your gift's ready. This was years later, and I'd tucked that promise inside a box along with so many of your souvenirs. When you'd call, you still talked to me as if I were the same age as when you left, as if, over here, time had stopped while over there, it kept tapping away at a normal rhythm. As if the hour time difference that separated us was expanding with each passing day and becoming a distance of years. You know, Mommy lives in the future. So when you said, Your gift's ready, you said it as if I'd just kept standing by the couch for years, staring at the front door. You said, I always wanted a tree as a gift, and when you said this, I imagined a Romanian tree arriving by mail, me and Dad staring, and the mailman saying, Where do you want it. And you kept on about this tree, saying that out in the country, when a child was born, the father and mother would plant a seed, and that seed would become the newborn's twin. So a child had a twin to talk to in the backyard, though luckily, they didn't have to dress alike. Then the child grew, as did the tree, and so it went for an entire lifetime, with the twin planted in the backyard and the child becoming a man, then an old man. After telling me all this, you said, But I couldn't plant a seed for you because we didn't have a backyard. Then you asked, Are you still there? And I answered, Yeah. Good, you said, and then, Because I have a gift for you that's worth a thousand planted trees.

One afternoon, sometime later, the gift arrived. I'd just come home from school, gotten off at my bus stop, fifty meters from the house. By the front door was an envelope for me, in your handwriting, with a mosaic of stamps from another country. I went inside, said, Hi, Emilio, and left the envelope in the kitchen. Is it from your mother? Dad asked, and I said, I think so. I put my backpack in my room, came out again, and Dad was sitting in the kitchen, in front of the envelope. Should we open it? he asked, trying not to sound too curious. So I opened it, and there was a letter from you and another envelope with a photograph inside. In the photo, you were standing in a field, hair blowing in your face, and beside you was a sign in the ground, and on the sign was written, Lorenzo. You were smiling in the photo, waving, and behind you was a river. The sign in the ground came up to your waist, the kind of sign that usually said, Keep out of the flowers, and there, instead, you'd written my name. Dad looked at the photo, looked at me, and then he said, Your mother's lost it. You explained everything in the letter, recalled the story of the tree, and that you'd bought me a small plot of land. You said buying land in Romania was like buying a gift that grew larger every day, because every day, that land grew in value. I looked at the photo again, that dirt field, the sign stuck there in the middle, the river behind it. At the end of the letter, you sent me a kiss, not even mentioning that you might return. Dad and I looked at each other, I tucked the photo and envelope away in the letter, and he said, Remember to call and thank her. I said, Do I have to?, and he said, Yes.

And so I started not wanting to talk to you on the phone, and when it rang at night, we'd make sure not to get there in time. Your monthly phone calls became biannual, then only to say Merry Christmas. And so Dad and I, unsure how to be together before, now wound up partners in our mutual disdain for you.

YOUR MOTHER SHOWED up at our house late one afternoon, before dusk. Dad's car was parked down by the sidewalk, the hood up, and the two of us halfway in, legs sticking out, the car devouring the rest of us. For a few days it had been hard to start, and that Sunday there was no getting it going at all. So we opened the hood and were busy unscrewing things and screwing things in, and Dad telling me, This is the radiator, here's the engine, and me asking stupid questions, because I'd heard people ask them, Are the fluids okay? Do we need to replace the fan belt?, and he always answered me seriously, as though my questions were valid, not just teenage blather. He'd say, Yes, I just checked the fluids, or, Yeah, maybe the fan belt went. While we were under the hood, we didn't notice your mother's car pulling up. But then we heard someone calling to us, saying, Sorry, and we looked up, Dad gripping his back and saying, Old age. A lady with coiffed blond hair had spoken from her car and now said, Sorry to interrupt, then told us she was looking for you. Dad wiped his sweaty forehead with his wrist, glanced at me, and said, Please come in, Ma'am.

And I met your remote-controlled brothers, too. They came in, one to the right, one to the left of your mother, both the same height, in similar clothes, wearing the same expression of two sons who'd grown up to be small-minded. And between them was your mother, who touched my shoulder, distracted though, looking all around. Your brothers shook hands with us, gave only their last name, the same last name. He must be Lorenzo, your mother said, pointing a boney finger at me, and they nodded and said, Yeah. Adorable, she said, studying the pictures on the walls, but still referring to me. Dad said, Please, and the three of them sat down on the couch. Dad and I shared the easy chair, with me perched on the arm. The first few minutes your mother spent talking with your brothers, as though Dad and I only happened to be there, and you'd arrive at any moment. Dad explained that you were in Bucharest for work and your mother said, When will she return, barely a question. I couldn't say, Dad answered, without anger, more to protect you from that shriveled woman than to complain about your being gone. Can you tell her we stopped by? one of your brothers asked. I can give you her phone number, Dad answered, but they pretended not to hear, went back to talking among themselves on the couch. I stayed on the arm of the easy chair, my hands filthy with motor oil, still wearing my cap to hold back my hair, which I was growing out. And I looked at your mother, her coiffed hair, her cheek folds dropping onto her red lips. Did something happen? Dad asked. Your mother looked at your brothers, then pointed to me and said, His grandfather died. She said it to be cruel, wanting to show how much she hated you, but there was only me to pile all that hatred onto, and me not even knowing what he looked like, this man she called Grandfather.

Dad phoned to let you know. I didn't want to talk to you, but I sat beside him. He told you your mother had come by with your two brothers, that they'd stayed only a short while, just to tell us your father had died. He said, I'm sorry, Lula, and I watched him and saw the sorrow in his eyes. The funeral, he said gently, they're holding it tomorrow. They wanted me to tell you. For a while he didn't speak, just held the receiver to his ear and stared down at the table. Then he hung up the phone without even saying goodbye. He got up to go outside, opened the door, closed it. I watched him out the window as he went to the car, opened the hood, and leaned inside. On impulse I brought the receiver to my ear, as though you might still be there. I sat at the table until evening, Dad not coming back in and me not able to go outside to be with him. Then I heard the engine turn over, and Dad came up to the window and tapped the glass. He came back, we had dinner, then watched some TV. Before we went to bed, he told me that when he let you know about your father, you'd stayed silent, just breathing hard. Then you started to cry and you didn't stop, until finally, you hung up the phone.

WE SPENT an hour looking for you, because Christian didn't remember where they put you and I never knew. We wound up in a long stretch of graves, all of them alike, Christian spinning around, hand shading his eyes, and the only thing he said was, Crazy. Then we split up, him on the right, me on the left, with him saying, You'll know it by her picture. We'd call to each other, in the middle of the gravestones, shouting, Did you find it, both of us answering, No, and going back to our search. Then I heard him call, She's over here!, as though he'd found you, lost, hiding, frightened in the corner. I shouted, Where are you? I saw him waving the bouquet we'd bought earlier. By the time I got to him, he'd set the flowers in the cemetery urn, the old flowers lying withered on the ground behind him. There you were on a square tile, a tile among dozens of others, all of them the same, a wall of the deceased, all democratically displayed in death, in the same squared centimeters. Christian was cleaning your picture like a father cleans his son's face, holding the boy still, wiping his mouth, the rest of his face, with a napkin. I'd never seen that photo of you before; you weren't young, as I remembered you, but you also weren't as you'd become. It was the point of greatest distance between us, perhaps even a moment when you were happy. You were laughing in the photo and wearing sunglasses.

Christian asked if it was okay to smoke and I said, I doubt anybody minds. We looked at each other, then at a gravestone in front of us. All just for one person, the dead man under there, a long gravestone, low and elegant. Practically a small house, while yours was a suburban condo. Christian sat down on the stone, thanking Mr. Petrescu, the name inscribed there. I sat down beside him. Did she smoke a lot? I asked, nodding my chin toward you. Yeah, he said, especially the last few years—after Monica arrived. He stared down at his feet, as if he felt ashamed to reveal anything about you, with you right there. But she did love you, he added. She just didn't have the courage to go back, he said, to face the two of you. So you talked with Christian. You told him things you couldn't tell me—on the phone you could only ask questions, get me talking, and then hang up. One time, Christian said, she bought a ticket to leave. She wanted to go back to Italy—she felt sick and betrayed. She didn't say anything because she wanted it to be a surprise. She packed, even put her apartment up for sale. While Christian spoke, he stared at the urn of flowers beneath your photo and sometimes glanced at me. But then the night before, she decided to stay—she just couldn't do it. So she went downstairs, took down the notice, and her apartment wasn't for sale anymore. The next morning, Christian said, I came to pick her up. I rang at the intercom and she said, I'm not going. And she didn't go, Christian concluded. He got down from the stone, took his wallet from his pocket, and pulled out an airplane ticket. It was faded, the date illegible. Here, he said, you keep it. I held it a moment. The destination had disappeared.

And the sun was slowly dropping, your photo devoured in shadow, darkness descending over the flowers now, and soon the two of us. Your sunglasses, useless now. What about your mom? I asked. In Spain. He spoke before I'd finished. She left after the revolution, he said, they closed the factory where she worked—my father worked there, too. Christian sounded detached, as though speaking of something far removed. I was still in school, he said. They were both glad Ceauşescu was gone, they were exhausted. Then they killed him, the factories closed, people were really scared. There was no work. They told us to wait, and we waited. But nothing changed and lots of people left, left the country to find work. We Romanians have always waited. We waited for the Americans for fifty years, you know. They never came. He slipped a cigarette between his lips, lit it. We're stupid, he said, we'll believe anything. Maybe we always trust the wrong people.

Christian got to his feet, We should be going. And I got up, too, and went over and cleaned your face. When I finished, I turned to Christian; he looked happy I'd done this. Should we write her something? he asked. I pulled out the ticket for the flight you never took. Might as well use it for something, I said. What should I put? Mama, he said, she knows Romanian. So I wrote Mama, and then we both signed it.

YOU COULD EVEN see the Ceaușescu Palace from your kitchen. Not so much the Palace but the light it cast, a glowing patch of sky. I woke up—it wasn't even four in the morning—I bolted upright in bed, unthinking. Waking up in your room, I was always struck by the smell of your blanket, your smell when you lived there. I went into the kitchen for some water, turned on the light, and there I was, reflected in the glass, squinting, in my underwear. To see Bucharest, I had to open the window, as though I had to let my reflected image out first. And I saw it wasn't true—that the lights don't go off all at once, at night. So maybe I was wrong. Outside was Bucharest, and only half the lights were off, a weakened city, some rows of streetlights still on and the rest turned off. Like planes taking off at night with only their courtesy lights on, until they reached their proper place in the sky.

Outside the air was still, arriving at the window but going no further. I could feel the air of Bucharest on my face, out the window on the seventh floor, and on my legs I felt the warm, humid air of your apartment, filled with my own night breathing, and with time. A bell rang that it was four o'clock, and I looked all around, trying to catch sight of a church, but I couldn't figure out where it might be coming from, that ringing of the hour. Ceauşescu, Christian would say, he hid the churches, surrounded them with buildings, a tooth pushing up where there already was one, widening, desecrating the mouth. Maybe the bells were ringing in there, some place I couldn't see, in among all those clumps of buildings. Ceauşescu, Christian would say, he actually raised churches and set them back down. And this was why you couldn't tell where time came from, when the hour rang. The first day, people looked around, puzzled, when they couldn't find the church, their expressions saying, Ah, this is nice. And that was Ceauşescu, Christian would say whenever he spoke of him or his palace or the churches or anything else about him. Then four-thirty rang, four tolls and one that was different, and again I couldn't tell from where. You used to say that we know where time comes from, and then you'd point to the church in front of us. It didn't occur to you that one night, someone might raise it, might bodily raise time, and set it down someplace else.

Then I left Bucharest outside; I shut the window, sat down at the kitchen table. At the center of the table was an ashtray, a drawing of the People's Palace at the bottom. I tried every kitchen drawer, searching for cigarettes—you must have left some. And so I found them, among plastic caps, rubber bands, a roll of tape, a few playing cards, a few stray birthday candles, probably inherited from the people living here before, a family with children. I took out one of the three open packs, two nearly full, one half-full, and I started to smoke. I ground my cigarette out on the Ceauşescu Palace, with it growing light outside and cars beginning to pass. An hour, and I wouldn't hear the church ringing out the time, I'd have to wait for night again, for it to sound. And so I got up, turned off the light, and headed back to bed. But by the door I noticed the large boxes I'd carried up, the ones you'd left at Viarengo's for years. I bent down, to go through them a little: I'd been walking by them for days, touching them, drawing back. Your name was written on each box, with a number beside it, as though you had some sort of order to abandoning your things. I ripped off the tape to one, opened it, then shut it again before seeing what was inside.

And then I loaded your boxes, one by one, back onto the elevator. I did it all very slowly, not wanting to be seen or heard. When they were all in, I pressed the button from the outside, and I let them go down on their own, with me tiptoeing down seven flights of stairs, and when I reached the bottom floor, the elevator was already there. I looked around, dawn coming, lights turning on in the windows. I carried the boxes to the dumpster, holding my breath, afraid of getting caught, like I was getting rid of your body. Then I stumbled, dropped a box, and it broke open. A small globe rolled out, not much larger than a tennis ball. It rattled onto the sidewalk. I picked it up—I hadn't realized you'd taken it with you. And I also didn't remember that we'd marked the globe with a pen. I'd asked you where Romania was, and you told me. I'd asked you where Africa was, and you told me. I'd asked you where America was, and the North Pole. And then I'd asked you where Via Colombo, our street, was, and you said, Here, and made a cross on the globe. But your hand must have slipped because seeing it now, that cross was below the bottom of Italy and above the top of Africa, in the middle of the sea.

A T THE BUCHAREST airport, people were looking up. An airplane couldn't land with the bad weather and was circling above the clouds. So everyone stood staring at the sky, but the only thing to see was clouds. By the time we parked, the plane had slipped through the storm, the passengers were safe, and everyone went back to looking straight ahead. Monica knew where to go; she made her way through the crowd, and I followed at her heels. They were at Arrivals, the men with their signs, and they pushed against the barriers as they waited for the door to open and spew forth the faces matching the names they'd written down. Then the door opened at last, the lobby was flooded with faces, and slowly, each sign secured its man. Monica smiled at some of them, one man stopped, shook hands with us, then left. The men she greeted were pretty much all alike, pretty much all like Anselmi. In their fifties, putting on weight, with a few days' growth, scuffed bags stuffed with Italian articles for their apartments. You could also tell them by their expressions, the way they looked around, arrogant and sated, with the self-importance of someone who's twice the boss for being in a foreign country.

The younger men, in contrast, hurried along, eyes determined but somewhat vacant, in nicer clothes, with a small carry-on and a computer bag. They saw Romania from above, as their plane descended, some only glancing up when the wheels hit the runway, gathering their papers together, slipping them into their bag. They worked for important multinational corporations, hundreds or thousands of Romanians slaving away for them day and night. They wore the same expression for the entirety of their brief stay, when they were picked up at the airport, transported, and shut up inside the company for a day or more. Once at the building, they attended meeting after meeting, projected transparencies onto walls, studied pie charts, checked the accounts, in their shirt sleeves, ties loosened, sometimes ranting, their thick hair a mess, their palms sweaty. For a day or more, they were up before dawn and at the company soon after, only leaving at night, brought back to their hotel, finishing their work in a T-shirt, laptop on the other side of the double bed. Then, business trip complete, there was always someone waiting for them outside the building, who got them in the car and brought them to the airport. When the plane took off and started to climb, they were back to their papers, wearing the same expressions they'd arrived with, expressions that had never left Italy, not for one second.

It took almost an hour for us to redo the ticket. Monica explained that the agency said we had to go to the airport to make the change. The girl in front of us typed on her computer, copying down information from the sheet we'd handed her. Then she looked past Monica and asked me, When? We stared at each other a moment, as if that question was somehow something between us. So looking past Monica myself, I said, Monday, and Monica turned to me and said, You sure? But I just said to the girl, An aisle seat, if you can. Then I took my ticket, and she went over it with me, pointing out the details with her pen. The lobby had emptied out, just a few men left with signs, three men pacing around, looking annoyed, orphaned by the people whose names they carried. Their signs were down now, like unused swords, basically useless, at least until the next flight. When Monica and I walked past, all three men held up their signs hopefully. I signaled no with one finger, the signs wilted, and the men went back to slowly pacing.

It wasn't raining out; the planes no longer had to circle above the clouds. Monica took my hand, and we walked along the fence. Then we stopped, and she put her fingers through the diamond mesh, as though she needed to hold on to stand. I did the same, as I'd done so many times before when I was little: now, my hands wouldn't go through. I felt something brush my legs—a dog. Monica was about to kick it, but I stopped her. Let him be, I said. The dog got up on his hindlegs, front paws against the fence as well. And at some point, the planes started to land, one after the other, practically in a line, and then they slowly slipped down the runway. Monica rested her head on my shoulder but kept her grip on the fence. So you're leaving, she said, and I didn't respond. I wish you wouldn't, she said. And then she started to count the planes landing. One, she said at first, and then, Two, and then they just kept coming.

FROM A DISTANCE, I couldn't tell what it was, that tangle of moving bodies. Then I realized they were tugging at someone, four of them, and a kid at the center. They were scuffling without a sound, with no sudden movements, shifting as one to the right, the left. I pulled up before reaching the warehouse, turned off the engine, and sat and watched. In Christian's car, empty cigarette packs were strewn everywhere; on the dashboard was the globe I'd given him, the one with the cross between Africa and Italy. I sank back into the seat, worn from Christian's back, which hadn't seemed so wide, until now. Then suddenly they were all shouting—the boy had slipped loose, took off running, the others after him for a few meters before they stopped. Now he was running past me, fifteen or sixteen years old, half-scared, half-mocking, laughing as he went. I got out of the car and went to join Anselmi's men, who nodded to me. One said, Asshole, pointing to the boy down the road. All four of them were in their work clothes; they spoke in Italian to include me. One of them said, Come and look, and he took hold of my arm. We walked beneath the flags, around the metal warehouse. On one blue side, Trăisască Ceauşescu was written in white, the paint dribbling down from the letters. I looked at it, and he said, It means, Long Live Ceauşescu. On the ground below lay the tipped can, in a puddle of paint.

By the time Anselmi joined us, all that remained of Ceauşescu was Ceau—one of the workers was washing it off, while the others sat in the grass, smoking and teasing him. It was a kid, said the one who knew the most Italian. He said this good naturedly, as if to say, The things kids do. Then he started to laugh. He had a strange way of laughing, with his eyes, squeezing them shut while the rest of his face remained still. Then he said, That boy has no idea who Ceauşescu was—he wasn't even born yet. Anselmi looked at the remaining letters, It's nice that way, he said, like a hello. Then he waved and said, Ceau, Ceau, and chuckled to himself. He turned to me, What're you up to? I'm here, I answered. Well, all right, he said, and he put his hand on my shoulder, then he steered me toward the road, alongside the warehouse in the grass and sunshine. He stopped, looking thoughtful, and turned around, shouting to the workers, What does Trăisască mean? Long Live, I answered. But Ceauşescu had vanished now, on the warehouse; they'd washed him away entirely, and all that remained of Trăisască was a T. Anselmi turned back around, put his hand on my shoulder again and said, Such strange people. Don't you think?

Soon we were sitting across from each other, the desk between us, with those papers on it that he'd showed me before. He said, I hear you're leaving, and I said, Monday. He said, So, did you think about it?, and I said, That's why I'm here. I looked over the papers, line by line, got to the bottom, and laid the pen on the desk. I'm not going to do it, I said. I'm not going to sell you her shares. Anselmi stared at me, and I watched his rage rising, flooding his whole body, up to his face. Then you have to stay here, too, he screamed, red and sweaty. But I wasn't listening anymore, I got up, left his office, went down the stairs, started across the lobby. Who the fuck do you think you are, he shouted from the mezzanine, and I waved goodbye. I heard him screaming until I was outside; I walked through the gate. I got to the car, rifled through Christian's empty cigarette packs, found one, lit it. I turned the car around at the gate, then pulled up beside Anselmi's four workers. I rolled down my window. And Ceaușescu? I said. All gone, they said, and laughed; one of them pounded on the hood. I rolled up my window. Village by village, I reached the main road. At the turn-off, I saw the boy who'd written the graffiti on Anselmi's wall. He looked distracted, thumb out, trying to catch a ride.

OUR LAST CHRISTMAS call came on New Year's. You called just after midnight, a coincidence. All you said was, Mom, as though you wanted to emphasize our bond, but at the same time, voice a complaint. I was in a noisy apartment, a crowd of people, loud music, and outside, fireworks going off in the dark. You said, Mom, and then you started coughing, and a bit warily, I said, Hi. In one ear, I had the roaring party, midnight laughter, and in the other there was you and all the silence around you, your empty home. I could hear sporadic explosions in the background, Bucharest celebrating the new year, but that silence around you was so complete, it was more like sniper fire at the window. You said, Mom wants to wish you a happy new year, and you coughed again, and kept on coughing, with me sitting on the couch next to a couple making out. I said, Happy new year to you, too, and then I pressed down hard on my ear because I couldn't hear you. I closed my eyes so I could focus on you, I squeezed into a corner, people coming and going, collapsing onto the couch, someone shouting at me, trying to get me to join in. On the other end, though, you were still there, speaking with some difficulty, inside that silence, tongue heavy from alcohol and sleep, saying, Mom's going to bed she doesn't feel well, in third-person, like adults use with children. Then you said, 'Night, and hung up the phone. And that was the last word I heard you say. 'Night, I answered, with you already gone.

The telegram arrived at the house one day when no one was there. My first name was on it, but the last name was yours; they'd slipped it under the door because the mailbox was so stuffed with junk mail. When I came in, I didn't notice the envelope, just stepped over it, hung my jacket in the foyer, then went to the kitchen. I ate, washed the two plates I'd used, went and lay down on the couch, walking by that envelope again without noticing. You were a thought I never had anymore, that only occurred to me now and then, like something having to do with someone else's life. At home, you never came up in conversation, either: Dad had taken your pictures down, and tucked them in a drawer. One of your weight-loss machines was still in the cellar—you'd kept it as a memento. It sat in one corner, and the only reason we hadn't thrown it out was that Dad liked to store some things inside so they wouldn't smell of mildew. Only your wardrobe was left untouched. It stood opposite the bed Dad still slept in, with one pillow, in the middle now. Your clothes hung inside; we'd had them cleaned, each item placed in a protective, nylon bag. All of them hanging in a row. Early on, Dad would air them out sometimes, hanging them all over the house, in the hall, the living room, the kitchen. They'd breathe for a couple of days, usually, and the house, at night, was like a field of crosses. Then we stopped airing you out; your clothes were left in their bags, and the wardrobe just stood there, an awkward presence at first, then later, like any other stuffed-full piece of furniture.

When Dad came home, I was asleep, face down on the couch. I heard his key in the lock and woke up; I stretched to pull myself out of my stupor, rubbed my face, swept back my hair. Hi, I said, and he greeted me as he walked by, returning shortly in his slippers. What's this? he said, handing me the envelope, then standing beside the couch. I sat up, looked at it, and said, Where'd you find this? There, he said pointing by the front door. I got up and went into the kitchen for a glass of water, then came back and sat down. Well? Dad said. I picked up the envelope, opened it, and read the telegram. Then I folded it in half, slipped it back in the envelope, and handed it to him. He stepped away from the couch and put on his reading glasses. Inside were the words, She has been taken from us, and the day of the funeral, and Anselmi's first and last name. After his signature, he'd added, My condolences, and again, for the second time, his first and last name. Dad put the telegram back inside the envelope and handed it to me. He didn't say anything. Then he let out a sigh, an enormous sigh. He let all the air out of his lungs in one long breath, then turned away, so I wouldn't see him cry.

I OPENED MY DOOR, and Dad didn't move, hands on the wheel, looking past the windshield. I patted his leg and said, I'll be back, like a hitman out to settle a quick score. I already had one foot on the pavement. I turned around but couldn't make out his expression: he was staring at the road ahead. He suddenly looked old. I got out, left the door open, and headed for the entranceway. I rang the buzzer with one finger, and kept pressing down until a woman's voice said, Who is it?, and then I stopped. Lorenzo, I said. The woman was silent a moment, the lock clicked, and I heard, Top floor, as the front door closed behind me. In the elevator, by the button, was a plate with your last name. I pushed the button, and the elevator broke free, a shot and a backfire.

Your mother stood at the end of the hall, a window behind her, a cutout against the light. I pushed through the glass door and walked firmly toward her, the maid trying to stop me, and your mother, taking shape, saying, Let him be. She waited where she was, the door shutting behind me, that endless hallway. I walked past doorways, rooms bursting into view. But I focused on your mother, her withered, sagging cheeks, that coiffed hair, unchanged over the years. She waited until I was standing in front of her, then she turned unsteadily, and I followed her into a parlor room filled with mirrors and couches. May I offer you something? she asked. No, I said and kept my eyes fixed on her, so I wouldn't look anyplace else. She sat down in the one armchair in the room, that spoke volumes about her isolation in her own home. I just stood there, looking down at her. From above, I saw gaps in that coiffed hair, her skull showing through. And Lula, she said uncomfortably, how is she? She's dead, I answered. Your mother looked down at her knees, not speaking, and I stared at those gaps. Then she nodded and kept nodding, and she looked up at the window. Yeah, she said.

When I got back in the car, Dad was just as I'd left him, hands on the wheel, looking straight ahead, motor running. I said, Done, and he said, Good, and released the parking brake, and we slowly drove away. So what'd she say? he asked after we'd gone for a bit. I told him she said, Yeah, and he looked at me and repeated, Yeah?, and started laughing, shook his head, said Yeah over and over, laughing, and I smiled, too, and looked out the window. So how's the apartment? he said, sarcasm in his voice. Big. Yeah, he snorted. But, really, I only saw the hallway to your home, the parlor and its couches, the light, all the silence passing through. Your mother didn't turn around as I walked out. I met the maid in the hall, a Filipino girl, who told me she'd show me out, and then went ahead of me. So I walked back down that long hallway, and the doors to the rooms had all been closed, to keep me from looking in.

Dad and I were just outside the city now, as we drove. I sat beside him, changing stations, and he stared straight ahead, once in a while repeating, Yeah, and smiling. Then we were at the airport, going up the elevated road for Departures, pulling between the other stopped cars. Dad turned off the engine, looked at me, and said, You be careful now. I looked at him and said, Don't worry. Then he said, I just can't, and I saw from his eyes that he was asking for my absolution. I said, This has got nothing to do with you, and I smiled. We'd been through this so many times before, saying our goodbyes, but those other times, it was you flying off and the two of us left on the ground below. Now I was leaving, I was the one going to the other side of the river, to see you put underground. Again, Dad said, You be careful, and then he opened his door and stepped out. He opened the trunk and pulled out my things, my backpack and roller bag. He helped me slip my backpack on, though it was small and fairly light. Then he smiled, ruffled my hair, and said, It might be time for a haircut.

I said, Yeah. He laughed and squeezed my arm. Standing in front of me, he was just like a father. I said, I'll call when I get there, and then I turned, and I heard the trunk, the car door closing, and then he was driving away.

I ARRIVED TO VIARENGO sitting on the low wall, a long
line of workers in front of him. They stepped forward
quickly, one after the other, and then they were gone,
getting on bicycles, mopeds, one in a car, kicking up dust. When
Viarengo saw me, he waved me over, like it was perfectly normal to see
me there. Here you are, he said, tilting his chin, looking at me from
under his glasses. Everybody shows up for payday, he said, laughing,
Look at 'em all. One after the other they stepped forward, Viarengo
picked up a packet of money, counted out the bills and handed them
over. Each worker took his money, put it in his pocket, said, Thank
you, and stepped out of line. Though every packet was bound and
ready to go, Viarengo took off the rubber band and recounted it every
time, then put the band back on and handed it over. Once in a while
he'd stop someone and start lecturing him, and the guy would lower
his head, wait for the sermon to finish, then take his pay and leave.
When Viarengo chewed out a worker, those standing behind him
would laugh and make fun of him, and sometimes there was some

shoving, and the whole line would ripple. I stood beside Viarengo and watched them come up one after the other, like he was handing out report cards.

So you're headed home, he said when he'd handed out the last packet of money. Yes, I said, I've come to say goodbye. Viarengo jumped down, adjusted his cap, and said, Good for you, this has nothing to do with you. Then he said, I almost forgot—I wanted to give you something. Come with me. We walked beside a warehouse, him in front, me behind. I watched him walking, his calves funneling down to his ankles, his back, neck, all the frailty of people from behind. We went through a door, actually, just a piece of nylon. So now you even get to see my warehouse, he said, waving to the sprawling room before us. There wasn't one open space, every meter piled high with all kinds of junk, bed springs, worn-out chairs, mattresses, bicycle wheels, a couple of old water heaters, some mirrors. Viarengo said, Wait here, and he walked into it all, as if diving into stormy sea. I saw him, and then I didn't see him anymore, he'd disappeared into mountains of junk, I could hear him shifting things around, letting curses fly. Look, he said, laughing, from behind a heap, holding up a portrait of Ceaușescu. Then he pulled out another, then another. They were pictures of Ceaușescu on his own, or with his wife, or hunting, or standing in a sea of flags and children. He showed them to me, then tossed them back into the pile, as if into a mass grave. He said, They were in such a hurry to get rid of these, but maybe they're worth something now. Then he was swallowed up again, and I heard, Ah, here it is. This must be yours, he said, holding up a sign, the kind seen in a flowerbed. The sign had Lorenzo written on it—the sign from the photo. You want it? he asked. I said, You keep it. To remember me by.

I walked toward Monica, waiting on the road for me, and then I turned to look back at Viarengo's ranch, the surrounding fields, and him in the middle of the road, watching me leave. Say hello to Italy for me, he shouted, and I waved, my back to him now. Monica started off before I shut the car door. Where do you want to go? she asked. Home. She looked at me and said, Are you mad about something? I looked out the window, at the fields ending as the city began, first everything flat, then everything rising, ten cement stories high. You think I'm a slut, she said, mouth twisted, angry to think it, disgusted to say it. No, I told her, and now we were entering Bucharest, and me feeling, truthfully, that I'd already left. It's because of your mother, she added, as if trying to shut down the thought that had come to her before. I turned to her, and suddenly I was laughing. What's so funny? she asked, both amused and offended. Sorry, I said, I don't know.

We said goodbye below your apartment, with her asking me, Will you be coming back?, and me answering, I don't know. I hope so, she said, and she kissed me, hard, her teeth grinding into my lips, her hands tugging my hair. Can I come up? she asked, and I said, No. She thumped me on the shoulder, tugged my hair again. Then she settled back against the seat, gave up, said, Sorry. I didn't know what to say in return, pressed against the seat, staring past the hood, at the brightly lit gas station in front of your building. Monica started to cry, sniffling, then sobbing, then blowing her nose in a tissue. Sorry, she said again.

WE LEFT AT DAWN; I found Christian waiting below, car windows rolled down and music rising from inside. He was sitting on the sidewalk and got to his feet when he heard the door click open and me come out. We greeted each other by the entrance, neither of us commenting that we were dressed alike, in a striped shirt and cap like we were about to go sightseeing, both of us in sunglasses. I tossed my pack on the backseat, shut the door, your name on the side, complete once again. Christian opened a map on the hood, said, Look, his finger to the map. This is it. He traced our route, twice, back and forth, It's not far, he said. Then he pointed to the river, said, It's past the Danube, and he leapt the river with his finger, as though it only took a nice hop to get to the other side. Great, I said, and we straightened up and looked at each other through our sunglasses.

In the photo you sent me, I could see the river. You were standing in a meadow with your wind-swept hair, and planted in the ground was that sign with my name. You were smiling, waving, and behind you was the river. One of the few photos I'd kept, and I pulled it out and laid it on my knees, then passed it over to Christian. He held it up on the steering wheel, drove a ways with it there, and out the window, the countryside going by, yellow flowers, horses bunched together. I stuck my arm out the window, felt the wind whistling over me, pushing me away. You once told me, That's what airplanes do, to slow down in flight, they go against the sky. And it was a game for us, you shouting, Help—the brakes aren't working, and both of us sticking an arm out the window, and going against the sky. And when we pulled our arms back in, we always had a few dead insects on our palms. I looked over at Christian holding the photo to the wheel with one finger and singing along to the radio. Then he handed the photo back to me. That's the Danube, he said, pointing to the river behind you.

We arrived and it was midday, a bend in the road, and the river burst into view, huge, wild. Christian parked by the bank, turned off the ignition. We're here, he said. So what do you think? Big, I said. We sat in the car, looking out, as if we wanted to plunge forward, the car slowly sinking down. He said, That's the land over there, pointing across the Danube, then opening the car door, getting out. We sat on the bank of the river, our legs dangling down, water rushing below our feet. Once in a while, a barge went by, loaded with gravel, slowly slipping past, endless, then after a time, returning, empty now, moving faster. Nearby, a man sat fishing in a small chair, pole at a slant, line lazily floating on the water. Christian said, If you want to cross, you have to take that. And he pointed to a small boat, a hundred meters down. It looked more like an old fishing boat, with a faded Romanian flag waving and a couple of people on board. Your mother, he said, looking at the boat, she only went over one time.

So you'd only gone over for that photo, that sign with my name on it. You went over like someone landing on the moon, who plants a flag, waves, and never returns. You took that boat moored just a hundred meters away, that flag waving even then. Slowly, you crossed the Danube, and first you stared at the bank you'd left behind, then at the bank coming closer. And in the end, you made it, over there. The spot I was looking at now, right there in front me, just on the other side of the river.

Afterword

This astonishingly powerful novel produces its unforgettable effects not through the narrator's thoughts or analysis nor through illuminating or thematic dialogue. I suppose careless reviewers might compare it to Hemingway, but the narrator is not tight-lipped nor stoic nor particularly brave physically, nor does the style, chaste though it might be, have the Dick-and-Jane simplicity Hemingway inherited from Gertrude Stein, her simple, repetitious, adjective-starved prose.

No, this heartbreaking book of loss and sullen, lonely maturity proceeds through its own devices, especially the careful, stripped-bare presentation of key visual images, which the reader must reconstruct (effortlessly) into a straightforward story. A young mother with a son, Lorenzo, gets together with a reliable, harmless man in order to provide the boy with a father—and eventually to free herself to become an entrepreneur with a more exciting partner in business and love. This enterprise takes her for longer and longer spells to Romania, recently liberated from its dictator, which people compare to the Wild West for its free-for-all competition and make-or-break economy.

As the book begins she has just died and Lorenzo, now an adult, goes to Bucharest for the funeral and to settle her part of the manufacturing business. Lorenzo has had no physical contact with her for many, many years. Now he learns she lived out the end of her life in squalor, alone and self-destructive, betrayed by her lover and business partner, who abandoned her for a younger woman. Only chance remarks fill him in on his mother's gradual degradation.

This novel, translated into English by Elizabeth Harris, comes to us covered with Italian prizes and the praise of such diverse writers as Antonio Tabucchi, Emmanuèl Carrére, and Michael Cunningham. Bajani, only in his mid-forties, has already written half-a-dozen works of fiction and a book-length essay, taught creative writing and worked for an Italian publishing house.

The stunning visual scenes include seeing the Bucharest skyline and the huge palace of the Parliament, The People's Palace built but never completed by the dictator Nicolae Ceauşescu, who ruled Romania from 1967 to 1989 and was executed along with his wife after a hasty trial (the last occurrences of capital punishment in Romania). Ceauşescu lived in another palace called "The Palace of the Spring," which was decorated in a style that might have appealed to Trump (huge gold-plated bathrooms and a Louis XV bedroom). The Parliament Palace is the heaviest building in the world and so large it can be seen from the moon, a Romanian chauffeur proudly claims. Lorenzo and the chauffeur tour the People's Palace; the guide deluges them with statistics (miles of marble, tons of crystal, etc). The grandiosity and cruelty and exaltation of those Christmas days of Revolution animate this novel. The Romanians are crude—"You Italians like Romanian pussy"—but the Italians are sometimes worse—"Did you ever ask yourself why your mother didn't come home? Did you ever ask yourself why?" Italian entrepreneurs despise the Romanian workers: "These people—we yanked them right out of the Middle Ages."

No reader of *If You Kept a Record of Sins* can ever forget the scene when Lorenzo is in the country visiting Viarengo, an Italian friend of his mother: "There before us was a meadow, and in the grass, a long stretch of coffins . . . laid in the sun, one after the other, like a battalion of dead soldiers, killed god knows where. They're all of the finest quality, he said. Same goes for the one I built for your mother, he added." Viarengo recalls that Lorenzo's mother liked to lie down in a coffin. "She'd say, Let's see what dying's like, and then she'd start laughing." Now Lorenzo climbs into a coffin and starts laughing; it feels as if he's playing with his mother again after all these years. Throughout the book Lorenzo addresses his dead mother as "you."

Lorenzo's boyhood memories are of his beloved but usually absent mother returning sporadically with souvenirs from all over the world:

"They were from every country, every corner on earth, my room, trip after trip, becoming the world map of your absence." Her weekly phone calls and monthly visits tail off; Lorenzo goes for years with only a phone call at Christmas from his mother.

Journalists say one can write better about a new city after three days rather than three months. It's true that observations are the sharpest after a very short time. Lorenzo is no exception: "All around was Bucharest, buildings of reinforced concrete crammed together along the boulevard, and a background noise I didn't recognize, as though even the traffic spoke a language other than my own." No wonder Bajani's technique of presenting strong visual images with a minimum of moralizing works so well; all of Lorenzo's impressions are fresh.

Edmund White

Acknowledgments

In a moment like this in which borders are more and more similar to walls, only stories still lack boundaries. They don't need an airplane or a passport: they just need people who love them, who care for them and want to carry them across an ocean. This is the way this story landed in the US, the oldest way in the world. I'm deeply and forever grateful to my publisher, Jill Schoolman, and the whole Archipelago crew, to Elizabeth Harris, who sang my words in a new language, to Jim Hicks and Anna Botta who started the book's journey across the ocean, to Beatrice Monti della Corte who helped me bridge the gap between Italy and the US, and to the American Academy in Rome, its directors Kim Bowes and John Ochsendorf and all the fellows and staff, who believed in me without knowing, at that time, how profoundly they would change my life.

—Andrea Bajani